FISH

A Novel

Owen B. Scott

Iophase Publishing

A Division of Iophase, Inc.

This is a work of fiction. Any resemblance to any person, living or dead, is purely a coincidence.

Acknowledgements

Many thanks go out to Webjorn E. and the rest of the Norwegians I worked with over 15 years ago, and who patiently taught me for a decade how to fish at the highest of professional levels, and virtually all of whom still fish, to this day.

Thanks to my wife, Lisamay, whose general patience with me and understanding of the realities of life has been an inspiration,

Thanks to Griffin, Jasper, Sully, and Ellany, and Crystal, all of whom inspire me to publish, and to leave something behind.

And thanks to Jonathan Raban, who stood on the deck of the F.T. American Empress in Seattle one sunny day in July and suggested I publish my experiences -- advice which took me more than 16 years to follow.

Finally, thanks to my parents, no longer here, but who always encouraged all of us to express our art in any way we could.

Prologue

The detective that had flown in to Dutch Harbor from Anchorage wouldn't let me wash the blood from my hands, either. "Forensics" was the word he used, which is what the local island cop in Dutch Harbor had also said, but with less assurance, when they first took us off the vessel.

There would be some lab work, he explained, in a dull, patient way, and apologized for the inability of the Dutch Harbor police to perform such work, at least to the satisfaction of the Alaska State Police. I was made to understand that all of this – the long interrogation in Unalaska, the hasty flight from Anchorage earlier that day, and my presence in what passed as a jail cell in Dutch Harbor -- even the handcuffs – they were all for my own good. His name was Chilton, and he was friendly.

"Custody," he said, smiling, "can be a benefit."

He wanted me to understand that I was not "under arrest" – I was, rather, being "held."

"This will soon be over." This I wasn't sure I heard him say aloud or if was a whispered thought inside my own head, since I had not slept in many, many hours. The doctor in Dutch Harbor, who was a kind old man recently arrived from Portland, Oregon said that I might not sleep for some time. That trauma such as that we endured could cause "hyper vigilance," which came with a laundry list of symptoms that I could look forward to, the comfort of sleep not being one of them.

Back in the room – I'll call it the "interrogation room" for lack of anything better – I faced Detective Chilton and another man across a wide folding table. The detective said, "Now we have to hear everything."

"But I've told it all on the island. Twice."

"I'm sorry. You'll have to tell it again. Start right from the beginning."

I looked out the window, but saw only the peculiar glow of wintertime Alaskan light. It was nearly noon, but the sun was barely hanging over the horizon, and looked like a silvery, worn nickel.

"The beginning of what?"

The detective stared at me. "Let's say the beginning of the trip." Tapping a finger on the table for emphasis, he said, "I need to hear everything that happened to you and everyone you know on that boat from the time you left Dutch Harbor three weeks ago."

I began the same way as I had twice before that day, and the room grew slowly dark with the telling.

"They made all fast throughout the ship, filled the mixing-bowls to the brim, and made drink offerings to the immortal gods that are from everlasting, but more particularly to the grey-eyed daughter of Jove."

Homer, *The Odyssey*

1

Twelve miles north of Dutch Harbor, at the entrance to the Bering Sea, a large pillar of black rock juts from the water like a sharpened thumb. It stands at the northwest tip of Unalaska Island, where volcanic cliffs rise straight from the water like the walls of a protected canyon. In 1778, Captain Cook reported seeing sea lions "guarding the harbor" at the base of the column. On the navigational charts the point is listed as "Priest Rock" for reasons long forgotten, but more informal names are often given by tired fishermen who see it after a long and hard trip in the Bering Sea. For them, it means a rest from a sea that can be many things, but that is mostly unforgiving, and in winter, usually brutal.

To the fishermen leaving the Aleutians heading out into the Bering Sea, Priest Rock marks the point at which their vessels must first stand against the weather. In the winter months even the largest factory trawlers should have everything stowed and lashed, since the storms come across from the Siberian coast one after another, until March.

I was a deckhand on the Northern Duchess. At two hundred eighty-seven feet long, she was one of the largest of the factory trawler fleet, and held a crew of about a hundred. It was early January when we cast the lines after a frantic, thirty-four hour "offload", where we unceremoniously dumped a thousand tons of frozen boxed fish onto the docks of Unalaska. Since we fished an "Olympic" fishery, where some thirty ships competed for a finite amount of fish, every moment we were not on the fishing grounds we were losing money. On that day in the early part of the month, in the height of the most lucrative season, where the fish were heavy with valuable roe, there was not a minute to lose. We were leaving Dutch Harbor straight into a raging storm. I checked my watch and found that we had about forty minutes to get the boat ready to take on the weather. We were behind.

The Norwegian bosun and I were clearing the deck of empty wooden pallets and cardboard, left over from the offload we had finished just an hour before. The wind had barely begun, but a steady stream of snow blew down to the trawl deck from above the protective bulkheads. There was no light except for the halogens mounted on the gantry and wheelhouse, and the snow had begun to stick to the frozen steel deck.

I glanced at the deck boss as he picked up a barrel of steel chain like it was a three year old child. I knew better than to offer help. At six-foot five and about two hundred sixty pounds, Vidar Tangen was every solid inch a classic Viking son. His long blonde hair was going gray. His beard was jagged and was covered with a fresh coat of breath-ice, and his face was worn down by twenty years of fishing in the North and Barents Seas not far from his home on the Norwegian west coast. His nose rested flat against his wide face, and there was a twist to his lips that had to have been the result of an accident. I had never asked him about it, and he had offered no information. The man had fished in the States for three years but he still had little English, and even though I had been his assistant for the entire time, we still communicated mostly with hand signals, although it was getting to the point where I felt I could read his mind. At the moment I knew he was wondering about the rest of our small crew. As was I.

I had to shout over a wind that had begun to howl, "Vidar, have you seen Taj!?"

The bosun didn't look at me. He shrugged as an answer, then he glanced around, hands on hips, to see what was left to do. Not much on deck, but we still had to fuel up the skiff before the wind hit us full force. Vidar climbed up the bulkhead to the level above that housed the small boat. I followed and saw that the straps that secured the skiff were loose, causing the sixteen-foot boat to rock back and forth as the Duchess plummeted off the top of each wave. I tightened the straps and Vidar stepped around me and into the incinerator room. He returned with a funnel and a five-gallon bucket of diesel fuel he had drawn. Then he saw the other deckhand, Taj, step onto the trawl deck with a pail of hot coffee from the galley.

"Ah, hello" Vidar said, addressing the coffee as an old friend.

The wind blew bullets of frozen spray into my face. I yanked down the hood on my deck suit. I felt like a rat peering out at a rising river. Then I saw Vidar take the coffee from my partner and direct him my way with a nod. The boss disappeared into the deck lounge just off the trawl deck. Taj bounded up the stairs, bracing himself against the wind. He smiled at me, wide and friendly. Tall, wide, but measured in all his actions, he was from the Samoan Islands, and he spoke with an island style of what appeared to be his own creation, and which changed as he saw fit, sometimes in the same sentence. Half of what came out of his mouth was Samoan proverbs, it seemed at times.

"Damnit, Fish. Man make me nervous. *Ua tulia afega.* "

I nodded. "He's a moody bastard for sure. But a hell of a deck boss, skill wise. You'll learn a lot. But don't push it – he'll come around. You just have to know how to take him. Best thing, 'til you get to know him, just stay out of his way."

He grinned. "Brutha, I got no problem with that. *Ou te se tagata tau suati.* "

Which meant, I had come to learn, something like "I'm the guy who stands on the outrigger." He seemed to say that one pretty often.

Taj, as we called him, was actually Tajaloaga Tanielu Simomea and he was new on the boat, and fairly new to fishing, but he was a good hand; bright, eager, likeable. In the island where he grew up, he started fishing commercially when he was eight years old. It wasn't clear how he had ended up in the Bering, but then those kinds of questions rarely came up. He was young, although he hadn't told me his age. I guessed it at twenty or so. Taj had a smooth, honest face and eyes that cut you in a nice way. His Creole was of an uneven type that could be turned off like a tap. He rarely sounded like a brother from the islands, most of the time like a San Diego transplant, and even times like a proper Englishman. It apparently depended on his mood. He was the only Samoan deckhand I had ever worked with, and I understood that he had suffered for a time on other, smaller boats, against the racism endemic to the fishing industry in Alaska, but on the Duchess he had found a certain balance. This would be his second trip with us, but his first with Vidar.

I lifted the bucket. "Hey Taj, help me with this stuff."

Taj held the funnel and I poured the contents into the tank. The wind blew bits of diesel all over the sixteen-foot boat. Once we reached Priest Rock, the job would be impossible. Four buckets later the tank finally overflowed slightly. It was the only way to tell when the skiff was full.

He began to wipe up the fuel. I said, "Forget that. We still have to put away the gangway and we need a little salt on the deck. And we're tryin' to outrun the wind."

We used the crane, which was mounted on the starboard side of the ship overlooking the trawl deck, to lift the long aluminum gangway. The last shift had hastily and somewhat lazily deposited in the middle of the trawldeck, and, being the night-shift, we were cleaning up after them. The wind blasted us in gusts of half-frozen spray. Cold, cold water. We had some luck, though. I drove the crane with a remote control strapped around my waist, and Taj guided the gangway into its cradle easily. Then he smacked it further into place with a sledgehammer and we tied it down with half-inch nylon rope. Since all of us on the deck crew had turned out early for our shifts to prepare the boat for departure, there was only the salt left to prepare the ship to face the weather.

We were fortunate on the Duchess to have a high trawl deck sheltered by tall bulkheads. That makes for a fairly dry workspace, but there was a mist blowing in and coating the smooth steel surface with a thin sheet of ice. The engineers wouldn't turn on the fire hoses until the fish processing factory started up, so we had nothing in the beginning of a trip to help us clear the deck of ice. It was my idea to use salt.

I waited on the trawl deck for Taj to appear with a bag. The wake of the boat leapt up behind us, white against the pitch-black water. The main engines screamed in competition with the wind, which now blew against my back, pushing me like an insistent friend.

Taj emerged from the deck shack with a fifty pound sack. By

some mistake we had ordered five hundred pounds of table salt, instead of the coarse variety. It was stored in bags in a room behind the deck shack, along with three thousand bags of sugar – sorbitol-- which was used in the manufacture of a fish paste the Japanese refer to as "Surimi". It was the primary product those days in the Bering Sea. Worth its weight in Yen, literally, since Surimi is the stuff used to make fake crab legs, and about a hundred other things in an industry that can always use a colorless, odorless, inert protein substance. Three thousand bags of sugar would last about three or four weeks. For the deckhands it was an inconvenience ro move and store them, although they had their various uses from our perspective. Often, when there was nothing to do, Vidar would nap in the sugar room, stretched out in a comfortable area he had cleared among the piles of fifty-pound sacks.

The salt spread out across the deck like fine snow.

"This won't last long, but it can't hurt," I said.

We used about half the bag and I tossed the rest into a small storage room on the port side of the deck.

"What's Vidar doing?" I asked.

Taj shook his head. "Nothin. Just sitting there at the table, smoking, drinking coffee. Brutha don't speak no words to me."

I said, "Vidar's the kind a guy you gotta draw things out of."

He pursed his lips and said, "No reason for me to draw nothin out of nobody. *Upu fa'aaloalo.* "

I smiled. Taj seemed to me to have as clear a view of the world as anyone I'd known. That and a sense of humor that'd make a snake laugh. The scary part was that I was already starting to recognize Samoan sarcasm.

We stepped into the warm deck shack. The place had been built as an area to store gear and tools, but we had turned it into a lounge. There was a picnic table slapped together from broken pallets surrounded by long benches covered with grimy foam cushions. The steel workbench now held a coffee machine, a microwave oven and a juice machine, all absconded from the galley over the past few years. There were Penthouse, Playboy, and Hustler magazines neatly stacked in old plastic milk crates resting on the floor. A life-size Bart Simpson doll hung by its neck from the ceiling with a perfect, thirteen-loop hangman's knot. Vidar sat at the table, nursing a huge cup of coffee and staring at the far wall. An unlit cigarette stuck out the corner of his face like a toothpick. He absently toyed with a piece of tarred black twine as he reached for a lighter on the table.

I threw my gloves into an empty milk crate and was about to sit down when the first major wave hit us on the port side, listing the boat twenty degrees in a violent whip like motion. Half a dozen empty and partially full coffee cups slid off the table. Taj managed to grab the coffeepot, which hadn't been tied down. I heard him yell, "Jee-sus!" We had reached Priest Rock.

Vidar sat like a chunk of stone, leaning slightly and unconsciously tilting his cup to compensate. We heard him mutter

"Fawn Skaerlings!"

Taj looked at me. I said, "It means 'fucking farmers'." It was about the worst insult Vidar could make against a couple of traditional Norwegian fishermen.

"He's talking about the guys in the wheelhouse," I explained. Then I said, "So who's driving the boat, anyway?"

Vidar said, "The captain, maybe?"

We laughed at the joke. Jon Elliot, the U.S. captain, was a "paper" officer. The year before last he had graduated from an academy in San Francisco. He was on board the Duchess by virtue of his license , his good looks, and the U.S. vessel-flagging law that required his presence. Now he was in charge of a forty million dollar factory trawler built three years before in Norway with money from Norwegian banks, but he wasn't really in charge of anything. In fact he was hardly allowed to touch the helm. At least not in a storm like that.

A sea from the opposite direction lifted the boat and slammed it down furiously. Water poured onto the deck from the top of the wheelhouse where a wave had crashed over. A loose roll of twine flew from a high shelf and landed next to Vidar. He threw it across the room.

"Tie this shit down." he said.

Taj blanched. The smaller boats he had worked on the previous year had hid from the worst storms. But there were few limits to the weather the Duchess would endure, and the forty-foot seas of that night were something new indeed. He looked up nervously at the wheelhouse.

I said, "Don't worry, Taj, we got some talent up there."

Vidar looked grim. "Gunnar Eriksen has no talent anymore," he said. This was an unexpected statement. It was one thing for a desk boss to call the Norwegian officers, otherwise known as the "fishmaster" and "fishmate," farmers, or some other pejorative term as a joke. But it was another for a Norwegian bosun to criticize the Norwegian captain in such a somber manner, especially in front of the American deck crew. Such was the atmosphere of cultural politics onboard this vessel, and all Norwegian-managed vessels in the Bering Sea. The American crew were generally present grudgingly, and only because of laws that demanded our presence. The Norwegians were the professionals in the factory trawler trade. They knew it, and especially in those early days of the industry, they never let you forget it.

Taj moved to tie down the twine racks. The deck boss sat before his coffee and brooded. Steam rose and mixed with the thick smoke from his cigarette. There was never a way to read the man from his expression, which had lost itself years ago among a maze of wrinkles and scars. Vidar was forty-eight years old, a living fossil among a pool of factory trawler bosuns in the Bering Sea. In the fishing towns on the west coast of Norway, he was a something of a legend. He had been on whaling ships as a young man, and I sometimes amused myself by imagining him stationed on the prow of an oar-driven longboat with a twelve foot harpoon in hand, scanning the grey waters for signs of fluke or waterspout.

I had developed nothing but respect for the man, despite his deadpan and gruff manner, but I was curious what Vidar had against Gunnar Eriksen, who appeared to me to be a friendly old Norwegian captain that the company had just hired.

"How long have you known Gunnar?" I asked.

The bosun didn't answer. Taj finished tying down the twine and returned to his seat, gripping the table. Vidar handed me his empty cup. I filled it obediently. After he had taken a drink and a pull from his cigarette, he answered my question.

"A fucking long time." The right side of this face pulled into a twisted grin. Unnerving at first, but I had gotten used to it.

"How long?"

Vidar hesitated, searching for the words in English. "Gunnar comes from the same island that I do. His family and mine have been fishing together for ... for forever."

He pulled a fresh cigarette from a pack and lit it with the end of the small butt still in his mouth. "And it has always been the same," he said, glancing toward the wheelhouse.

"His people upstairs ... my people on deck."

There was a pause, and then I said, "You've been fishing for how many years? Why not go and do what it takes to get a job running the boat, then?"

He smiled faintly. "It doesn't work that way. Sometimes, maybe.

Not in this life."

We listened to the wind and sea for a moment. Then Vidar said, "That's fine, but who knows more -- and who knows what to do when the... shit happens? When things break, when the fish go away?"

I shrugged. "Gunnar runs the ship. He's in charge."

Vidar scowled and pulled from his mug. "Yes, oh yes. The fishmaster is always in charge, but a smart fisherman listens to advice from the bosun." He gestured toward the trawl deck. "We know what the hell is going on out there. We're closer to it. "

"And so Gunnar doesn't listen to you?" I had learned more about Vidar in the last ten minutes than I had in the previous two months, and I wanted more.

Vidar lit another cigarette from his inch-long butt. "Gunnar's father was smart. My father worked for him. Old Eriksen listened to my father and they pulled a lot of fish out of the North Sea." He laughed shortly and said, "Maybe too much. That's why we're here now, eh? Doing the same damned thing."

We smiled. His blue eyes were liquid and bright in the neon light. It occurred to me for the first time that maybe Vidar had smuggled a bottle of something or other onboard. He had never been so voluble. His mood had become lighter but now a shadow passed across his face. He said, "Those men are dead now. They were friends, and I think Gunnar and I pretended to be friends ... for them. Their memory. But we don't pretend anymore."

He was quiet for a moment then he sighed and said, "Gunnar has a different style. He likes the glory of finding and catching the fish alone. But when things go wrong, he suffers alone, too."

We listened to the drone of the engines, the wash of the spray against the upper decks. The ship shied like a nervous pony. Taj was developing a focused look of nausea, and stood up to retire to the bags of sugar. Looking at Vidar's response to the weather, we could have been on the Staten Island Ferry.

I said, "Well he must be pretty damn good if they hired him. This boat broke a world record last year. They're not gonna let some greenhorn run it."

Vidar said, "He's not a bad fisherman, but I don't think you understand what I mean. Gunnar is the last Eriksen to fish. His father is gone. His brothers have quit. His sons refuse to fish. They sell insurance in Alesund. He's lost his reason to keep going. This is maybe his last shot. I think he's finished. But we'll see."

I filled my cup and returned to my seat. I noticed that the motion of the boat had changed, become steadier. Whoever was running the ship had turned it into the weather and slowed it down. It rode the long swells head on, pitching fore and aft like crazy, but not rolling more than a few degrees. In a vessel like ours in seas like those, the rolling is the worst of it. And the most dangerous.

"What about Gladsjo?" I asked.

"Martin's a good fishmate," said Vidar. "But he's not ready yet to be a fishmaster." He stared at me over his coffee. "You know Martin well enough."

I did. Vidar knew he was my friend. I said, "He has a U.S. mate's license."

The old man smiled. "Saves the owners a lot of money."

"Why?" Taj asked.

"In this company," I explained, " the U.S. officers are hired for their licenses, to comply with the law. For every officer, there is a Norwegian counterpart to do the fishing, an 'advisor'.

A Norwegian fisherman with a U.S. license can fill two positions. And Martin is a U.S. citizen. He was born in Seattle."

"But he lived his life in Alesund," said Vidar.

"Right. And now he lives in Seattle again. I don't think he's going back home."

The intercom rang. I pressed the green button and a voice came over. "Paul Saxon? You there?" It was the captain.

"Yep," I called to the monitor, "What's up, Jon?"

"Fax from Seattle."

"Okay. Thanks."

He rang off and Taj said, "That man's 'bout the only one on the boat don't call you Fish."

I shrugged. "No nicknames in the academy, I guess."

"Aye aye," he said.

On the way to the wheelhouse I took the starboard side ladder to hide from a wind that was blasting the Duchess from a few degrees to port. Even on the lee side I had to struggle against the wind to open the hatch to the house. The bridge was silent and dark, lit only by the glow from the radar and plotting screens.

Gunnar was hunched over the chart table, a pair of reading glasses on his nose, his paunch slipping over his belt. His heavy jowls and shock of gray hair were illuminated by the chart lamp and he turned for a moment, grunted a greeting and again peered at the charts, as if the fish would magically appear as tiny black dots. if he stared hard enough at it

"How far, Gunnar?" I asked.

He didn't look up. "We'll be fishing in four hours, I think."

"You hope," said a voice from the shadows. It was Martin. He smiled as he swiveled in the captains chair. He must have taken over when Gunnar went to consult the charts. "Hello, Fish. How's it going out there, eh?"

"Fine, Martin," I said to my friend.

Five years before, Martin Gladsjo had been a deck boss on the company's first boat, the Northern Resolute. At the time I was a green, but enthusiastic processor more-or-less happily engaged in a brain-dead job below decks in the fish factory. I would sometimes come up to the deck shack during breaks and play chess with Martin, who fancied himself a formidable player, at least until he met me. My father sat me down with a chess book when I was eight and we ran through the openings for a year before I could beat him. I lost to Martin maybe twice in three months, but he got better and better, and never complained about losing. During those games, Martin apparently noticed enough of a certain quality in me to arrange for a trial trip on deck as a "combi," short for "combination" to mean part-time in the factory below decks and then up on the trawl deck when needed. The factory manager was reluctant to let me go, but Martin was persuasive.

When the first wave swept over the stern and caught me in the waist during a weather-beaten haul-back I knew from the bottom of my soul that I had found a career. What he had seen in me showed itself almost immediately, and within two month-long trips I became a full-time deckhand.

I did well under his style of tutelage, which was the opposite of Vidar's. Voluble and articulate, he explained the trade to me in excruciating detail as we brought up one 100-ton bags of fish after another. His command of English was flawless, since he had an American mother. His Norwegian father had taken the family to the west-coast fishing city of Alesund when Martin was a baby. He had returned to America at the age of twenty-seven for the first time to work on the Resolute as a deck boss.

When the company built the Duchess, and I heard he was to be the fishmate, I pulled every string I had in the office to follow him to the new ship. It had been a good move. I flourished on the Duchess, gaining a solid annual contract and a promotion to assistant bosun. All along the way Martin had been there, encouraging, smoothing over the worst of times, celebrating the best. Last year the Duchess had caught forty-two million dollars worth of fish. Smashed the world record. Martin proved himself to be a hell of a fishmate. Now he was just a step away from running the most successful fishing vessel on the globe. In our own little universe of the competing factory trawlers in the northern and southern seas of the world, we were stars.

I looked through the dark windows at tiny points of light bobbing wildly on the horizon. Other fishing boats leaving or returning to the islands. The sea slapped against the glass, and I gripped for a moment the edge of Martin's chair. High in the wheelhouse of the ship was where you most felt the violence of the sea. I said, "Nice storm, Martin."

He grinned as if he had ordered it himself. "Love this weather. Makes life worth living, eh?"

I thought about the seventy processors strapped in their bunks, probably puking green and yellow bile. The worst nausea imaginable.

"Some people downstairs might not agree," I said. I looked around the bridge. The long, leather-upholstered couch in the corner was empty. "Where's Jon? He said I had a fax."

He nodded toward the radio room, off the port corner of the wheelhouse. The room served also as the business office of the ship. There was a desk, a fax machine, a satellite phone and a computer. Jon was at the computer, playing a jet-fighter simulation game. I stepped in and looked over his shoulder.

Without looking up he said, "Bombing the shit out of Baghdad! Gotta watch those... ouch." He sighed. "Lost one." He looked up from the game. The pure, smooth face of a boy stared up me. Clean-shaven, deeply tanned, perfect teeth. Light blonde hair, pale grey eyes. Would be more at home, I thought, on a beach at Malibu. It was hard to take him seriously as the captain of a 5,000 gross-ton factory trawler pushing out into the wintertime Bering Sea, yet he carried with him an aura of innocence that was impossible to dislike. And he seemed to harbor no resentment regarding the limitation of his position. Which was why he was still employed, I thought cynically. His face turned serious.

"Everything secured?"

I suppressed a smile. Aye aye, el capitano. What would he look like with epaulets, I wondered. I said, "Yep. Ready to go." He gave me a thumbs-up and sat for a moment, perhaps trying to recall a reason for my presence, when it dawned. "Oh yeah, Paul. A fax. Your wife sent a fax."

"Ex-wife."

"Ah. Right. Ex. Sorry."

I shrugged. Somehow I always felt brusque around the guy. I read the fax. Folded it up and slipped it into the pocket of my deck suit.

Jon stared at me expectantly. As if you didn't already read it, I thought.

"She found out about my raise last week. Wants more child

support."

He nodded sympathetically. "She must have a pipeline to the office," he said.

I nodded. "It's okay. I was going to tell her. I don't care about the money. She and Sofie need it more than I do."

An old story. Nearly every one of us Americans who had been fishing for more than a few years were divorced. The Norwegian culture had apparently long ago absorbed the concept of prolonged absence. The American response was completely understandable, given our general attention span, our distaste for commitment. Understandable, but no less painful.

Stephanie and I were married four years before, just after my first year at sea. I first met her on the Resolute, and we worked side by side for a year. But we didn't fall in love until we walked around Dutch Harbor in the rain one day, playing like children in the muddy, endless roads. It was a hopeful and happy time. We bought a small house in West Seattle with the steady chunks of cash from fishing. We returned from Alaska one October to discover she was pregnant. The following summer Sofie Miranda Saxon was born. I thought that she was the most beautiful thing I had ever seen.

But with my promotion came new responsibilities. I was expected to spend more time at sea, and would be called to Alaska without warning to replace a deckhand that had gotten injured or quit. Steph began to tire of having a part-time husband, a part-time father for our daughter.

Before we celebrated our second anniversary, she had delivered an ultimatum. I wavered, and Steph, never one to play games, filed for divorce. The man who delivered the papers in Dutch Harbor also delivered a message from Stephanie: if I flew home and quit my job, she would withdraw the papers. Gripped by a certain type of inertia as strong as any current, and considering the loss of the sea all around me on a daily basis, and what that loss might do to me, to my family, my child, I signed them.

It occurred to me that I had forgotten to take off my deck suit. Not very polite of me. Jon noticed it too, and was staring uncomfortably at the dried fish slime that covered most of the suit. If there was a refuge from the muck and blood and death of a fishing boat, it was there in the warm and carpeted wheelhouse.

On my way out I glanced over Martin's shoulder to look at the video monitor that depicted the ocean bottom. Tiny dots of red registered fish in small patches throughout the water column. -- "sign," as it was called.

"How's the sign?" I asked. Gunnar, who had now taken the chair on the other side of the helm said, "Nothing to drop a net onto, that's for sure."

Jon had followed me out and looked at the screen as well, screwing up a face of concentration. He pointed at the top layer of sign, which was greenish, and thin.

"Ghost sign, right?"

Martin said, "Probably. Feed. Little fish."

Jon nodded seriously. Martin stole an amusing glance in my direction. Gunnar appeared to be absorbed in a kind of Nordic trance, staring out at the black. A deep southern drawl with a French twang boomed through the intercom.

"Captain Elliot ... are you there?" It was the steward.

Gunnar leaned into the monitor. "Hey cook, what is for dinner this evening, please?"

A wheezy laugh drifted through the intercom. "No potato balls tonight, Gunnar. Next Thursday. Jon... what would you like for dinner?"

Anton Gastineau, or Tonni, was the only one of the key crew who held fast to the antiquarian protocol of treating the licensed captain of the ship as royalty. Dinners were delivered to the wheelhouse, where the captain dined in solitude. It was the only time the captain was left in command of the bridge , except for appearances sake in the harbor, when the Norwegian fisherman typically vanished for about thirty-six hours.

Jon said, "What have you got, Tonni?"

"We have blackened cod or spicy chicken tonight, captain,"

Tonni recited, "Unless you'd like to go vegetarian. We just left Dutch, so I have plenty of fine vegetables."

"I'll have the chicken, Tonni."

"Very good. Coming right up, sir."

Martin stabbed at the red button on the intercom and said, "Vegetarian? On a fishing boat? What the hell?"

Gunnar shook his head. "I like his potato balls, but that is one strange American."

Tonni was immensely obese, and spoke with a lilting Cajun quality that left him breathless between sentences. He was entirely bald and wore a heavy earring in his left ear, which he toyed with incessantly. He had an effete manner that recalled old interviews with Tennessee Williams.

"He's from the south," I explained. "New Orleans. I guess he was quite a chef down there. Wouldn't know it now."

Captain Jon shot me a look. "I like his cooking," he said.

I felt foolish for a moment. I hadn't meant to put down the cook. It seemed childish to pick on someone so eccentric. A bullying trait I imagined I was picking up after years of life on the boats.

We looked into the wet night before us. It is always a measure of your status on any fishing vessel by how many minutes at a time you feel welcome in the bridge. Of course you must take into account the mood of the various masters. If the fishing is very bad one is wise to avoid the place altogether. In this particular case I had reached my limit.

Downstairs Taj had just returned with another pot of coffee to fill Vidar's bottomless stomach, but the boss was nowhere to be seen.

Taj shrugged. "He was here when I left. Hey Fish, you been in the galley tonight?" His eyes were lit with excitement. Young

Taj. Cracked me up sometimes.

"Nope."

"Then you haven't seen her. My God, Fish, wait till you see what they sent up as a galley assistant. Aiiiii-ya! *Matagofie!!*"

"A woman, I take it?"

Taj's lips were pursed, eyes closed, visualizing. "Oh, oh, oh" was all he said.

I shook my head. "Chrimany, Taj."

Tonni's enormous bulk appeared at the entrance to the galley. He called across the deck, "You boys going to eat, or you goin' to fuck around all night?"

I held up an arm. "Thanks. We'll be in."'

Tonni said, "You and the engineers are the only ones up. Processors are all in bed. Offload beat the shit out of 'em. Hah!"

Taj followed him inside. I looked out at the deck. Waves were tonguing their way over the stern. The salt was long gone. A layer of ice had begun to form across the steel, but was broken up here and there by rivulets of water. The boat fell away beneath me with every long swell, then came to push against the soles of my boots, a comfort. It feels good when a ship you trust is alive beneath you.

2

Taj was not exaggerating. She was lovely. About five-three, smooth and olive-skinned. Hair and eyes as black as the sea outside.

She looked part Hawaiian. She was also very, very sick. She stood behind the food counter, leaning on the stainless steel, looking like she was going to throw up into the soup. I took a plate and bent down a bit to catch her eye through the Plexiglas. I smiled. "Hell-o up there. You okay?"

She wasn't, not even close, but she managed a tight grin.

"Who are you?"

"Just call me Fish."

"Fish? Are you kidding?"

I shrugged. "Nickname. Never get rid of it. Not up here, anyway. And you?"

"Alani."

I gestured toward the blackened cod, handed her my plate. She lifted the fillet like it was a dog turd and set it next to my dinner roll. Without my asking she added an ear of corn, but I noticed her eyes had begun to water.

"Excuse me," she said, and handed me the plate before she ran into the galley. I could hear her retching into the sink. Taj appeared at my elbow, grinning.

"Have some pity, asshole," I said.

"She need more than pity, Fish."

We finished filling the plates ourselves. Tonni appeared at the door and I heard him say something about patches. I set my plate on a table Taj had picked out and went into the galley. The place was trashed by the weather. Stainless steel trays everywhere, silverware and plastic cups scattered across the floor. She was leaning into the sink and Tonni stood by the stove, looking flustered.

"Fish, be a good boy and run up to the wheelhouse and get some patches for this poor darlin'. We got the food out, now we just gotta clean up this place."

I shook my head. "No patches, Tonni. She doesn't need that garbage."

In dire cases of seasickness you can place a cloth patch treated with scopolamine on the back of your neck and wait for the chemical to seep into your system. But the drawback is that scopolamine is a powerful drug that has side-effects that are sometimes worse than the seasickness. And once you use up a patch, you have to use another to keep the nausea at bay. And so forth, sometimes for weeks. If you have some patience and wait it out you'll be fine in a day or so.

I placed a cool hand on the back of her neck. She rested one of hers on mine. Grateful for the simple gesture. Sometimes people needed to be touched. I spoke into her ear. "First   time out?"

She nodded. I said, "You stay right here. I've got something that'll maybe help."

I didn't like to enter my cabin in the middle of a twelve hour shift. It was eight-thirty at night and I wanted to avoid waking up my roommate. But then I remembered that Rusty, who was the deckhand in my position on the opposite shift, had shared a bottle of something with his partner during the offload. He wouldn't be waking up. I slipped into the room and heard his deep snoring. I found my stash of peppermint tea and a small bag of ground, dried ginger. It was my little secret that I, too was sometimes nearly incapacitated by seasickness.

Back in the galley I prepared a hot drink made of the two ingredients. I steered her into the empty TV lounge and placed the drink in her hands. Tonni followed me in.

"You just let Dr. Saxon take care of you, honey."

I said, "Sip this, Alani. Stay quiet in here and try not to heave it up before it settles your stomach. And breathe the steam, too. Always makes me feel better."

"Thanks." She managed a smile. I closed the door softly behind us.

In the mess room Tonni turned to me. "You a good boy, Fish. But maybe this trip you try to keep your penis in your pants."

"Tonni, give me a break."

"You know what I mean."

I did know. I read somewhere that promiscuity is common after divorce, an affirmation I have taken to heart. Apparently I was developing a reputation. Four girlfriends within a year on a boat where maybe one-fifth the crew is female.

But on a factory trawler casual sex is a way to push against the unfathomable emptiness of a grey, stone-cold sea everywhere around you. A percentage of the crew changes every three weeks, so the opportunity for new, fleeting romances comes around often. And there are the circumstances of my particular niche: a high-profile job in a closed, feudal setting. Feudal in the sense that if the masters in the wheelhouse can be thought of as kings, the processors are certainly serfs, the deckhands, gracious knights. An odd, but fairly accurate metaphor. There are only eight of us. We are dressed in bright red single-piece suits, and are armed with knives strapped at our waists. We wage a constant battle against events that conspire to prevent the ship from bringing forth a thousand tons of fish a day. We are the most visible breadwinners of the crew, and what's more, maidens fresh from the mainland are free to watch us in action from tall windows in the wheelhouse. It's the best show on the boat, because it is real, and dangerous.

Tonni stood before me, smiling, touching the giant silver earring. At times he seemed distressed by what he referred to as the ship's "Moral Laxity."

I said, "Don't worry about me, Tonni. I'll worry about me. Besides, I'm busy with a project this trip."

He cocked an eyebrow. "Oh?" he wheezed. "Another long, impossible book?"

I smiled. Tonni was perhaps the only one of the crew with whom I could have this type of conversation. I said, "Proust."

"Proust! Hah!"

The day before I flew from Seattle I had found a set of "Remembrance of Things Past" in a used bookstore for eight dollars. It was resting on a shelf in my cabin in a slipcase, gathering dust. I had been fishing a month and had not cracked a volume.

"I'll get to it."

Tonni winked. "Better off if you get to Alani. You're too young to read Proust, son." He looked down at my plate. "Eat your dinner, Fish. It's getting cold."

Taj had almost emptied his plate. The mess room was nearly empty. Gunnar, Vidar and Martin sat at a table in the far corner. I sat down next to Taj and a processor whose name I never got. But he knew me, apparently.

Taj said, "Is she a babe, or what?"

I nodded. "She's a babe, all right. Lost in the woods."

The blackened cod was good. Tonni was best at his native

specialties.

Taj asked, "What net we usin?"

I looked over to the Norwegians. Martin was talking quickly, gesturing with his hands. Gunnar and Vidar looked coolly on. There was no evidence of acrimony between the two older veterans.

"I guess they're cooking that up right now." I looked at my watch. "Whichever net it is, we'll shoot about midnight, I think. Our shift will set, but we won't haul back."

"You don't think we'll have fish by two AM?"

" I Hope not. Like to get in a nap."

Taj shook his head. "Gettin old, Fish."

I stretched. "You better believe it, pal. Twenty-nine is old in this business."

The processor looked up from his meal. "You ever been hurt, Fish?"

I hate that question, because it always leads to an explicit conversation about injuries on deck -- mangled hands, broken arms and legs, crushed skulls. Seemed like I'm the only one who can't stand to talk about it, especially when I'm eating. I looked at my hands. Intact, still. All body parts still present, in fact. No broken bones, maybe two, three close calls in five years. That was it.

Otherwise, an absolute blast of a time, thrill after thrill.

Like a kid on a jungle gym addicted to adrenaline. Using mind and body to make split-second decisions. I can't think of a better job than one in which you are faced daily with your own mortality.

I said, "Couple of close calls. That's all." I carefully touched the thin strip of oak trim around the top of the table. Fishing has made me superstitious.

The processor began eagerly, "I heard that there was a guy on the Saga Clipper--"

"I don't want to talk about it, bud," I snapped.

He shut up. "Okay. Sorry, man."

I waved a hand at him. No big deal. I returned to my cod. The processor got up and left the galley.

A thin man in crisp blue coveralls stepped into the mess room, pulling at a long, combed beard. His curly head of hair framed a set of round glasses resting on a sharp beak of a nose. The man walked past the food, gave a cursory glance in our direction and stepped into the galley, calling for Tonni. Seconds later he returned with a fistful of bananas.

"Oh, shit," said Taj. "Here come Hastings."

Taj turned as the tall man approached the table. Hastings threw the bananas on my empty plate and said, "Every time you fucking primates break something out there, you get some bananas. Here's some now. Feeding time."

I looked at the bananas. Then up at the tall, bony man.

He pointed at Taj. "This idiot and his sidekick managed to destroy the hydraulic motor on the aft crane this afternoon. I'll let him tell you about it." He stalked off and sat down with the Norwegians.

I sighed, and looked at Taj. "What happened?"

He said, "The combi was swinging a load too fast, didn't shift the boom in time. Fool smashed into the side of the gantry."

"The "combi" was driving? What were you doing?"

"Hooking up the loads, giving him directions."

"Geez, Taj."

"I thought he needed the practice."

"Evidently, he did. Look, if you're going to train a guy, you let him move empty barrels around an open deck or something. When there's nothing going on. You don't hand him the controls during an offload where everyone's in a panic to get the boat unloaded."

Taj nodded. He knew how to take it, as it flowed downhill.

He said, "Felt sorry for the kid, jus' stand around all the time, watchin'."

I said, "Shit, let him stand. He probably needs the practice."

I looked over at the table, where Hastings was describing the accident. I muttered, "Now we got the chief freaking out."

"The chief is a scumbag," the Samoan said, in a low voice. "Some kinda flaked-out computer geek. Why's he comin at you, anyway, Fish? Vidar's the boss."

"You think he's going to throw a bunch of bananas on Vidar's plate? Hastings knows he can say anything he wants to me. Anyway, I'm supposed to be responsible for you guys, more or less."

"Sorry I let you down, man."

"Ah ... " I made a dismissive gesture. "When you're done

maybe you can find this combi, go out there and help Hastings with the crane. What's this guy's name, anyway?"

"Dave or Steve, or somethin'. I'll get him. Fool's probably asleep. Processors pulled thirty hours straight, you know."

"Too bad," I said. "Maybe he'll be more careful next time."

Taj left and I let the anger dissolve within of me. I was as irritated with Vidar as much as anyone. It seemed like he was slipping further away from the details of his job, leaving me to fill in the gaps. I glanced over and he was looking at me, amusement in his eyes.

His voice reached across the mess room. "Fish, why did you hire a brain-dead combi?" The table burst into laughter. Hastings' grinning face appeared over Vidar's shoulder.

"I didn't hire anyone," I shot back "You hired him. Anyway he's a relative or something of Tonni's." Tonni entered the mess room.

"And a very fine young man. You take care of him, Fish."

"He'll have to take care of himself, Tonni."

Tonni sat down. "Aw, lighten up, Fish. He put a sweaty hand on my arm. "What's bothering you, boy?"

I pulled my arm away. "Nothing. What's this guy's name, anyway?"

"Stephen. Stephen Girard." He leaned forward. A drop of sweat fell onto my plate. He whispered, "He's had a very hard life, Fish."

I looked at Tonni. Taj appeared and said, "He's not in his room."

Tonni said, "You mean Stephen? He's in my room, watching a movie, I think."

Taj left and the chief got up and started for the door.

I said, "Those guys'll be out there to help you, Hastings."

"Good," he said.

I watched him walk out of the mess room. I said, "Tonni, will you get rid of these goddamned bananas, please?"

I filled my mug and sat down next to Vidar. Alani came out of the TV lounge looking a little better and scooped up my empty plate on her way to the galley. She smiled over her shoulder as she went by. Actually, she looked a lot better. But I knew that the cure was only temporary. I would bring her more later, after my shift.

I would never get to Proust this trip, this much was clear.

I said to Martin, "How is our fine chief engineer this evening?"

He smiled. Martin had a pleasant face, and light brown hair that was, I noticed, beginning to thin after three years in the wheelhouse. His face had filled out and a slight paunch was starting to push past his belt.

He chuckled as he said, "Hungry for power. He begged for two years for a fax machine in the engine control room. The office finally sent one up. Now he can talk to Seattle, to other boats. He doesn't need to come up to the bridge anymore."

Gunnar spat out his toothpick. "Power! Hah! I should like to give him some power right on the nose!"

Martin smiled. "Everyone wants to run the ship. But there can be only one captain at a time."

Gunnar looked away.

Vidar said to me, "You don't have to listen to this guy Hastings, Fish. He is just a chief engineer."

I shrugged. "And I'm just a deckhand. Why fight people? Wouldn't it be easier if we just got along?"

"But we don't," said Vidar shortly.

Martin said, "You are too nice a guy, Fish."

"That's a laugh. I just laid into Taj a little while ago. Felt like a real nice guy then."

"That's part of the job," Martin said patiently. "A deck boss is supposed to bitch people out."

I looked at him. I appreciated the sentiment, but I said, "I'm not a deck boss. And I don't see Vidar screaming at anyone."

Vidar picked up his empty soda can and crushed it like a piece of paper. When he opened his huge and twisted hand the can was a ball about the size of a tangerine. He threw it on the table.

"I don't scream," he said.

Gunnar grunted and left with his coffee cup. Vidar suddenly looked embarrassed, picked up the ball and tossed it into the garbage.

3

We set the gear at 1 A.M. The "sign", Gunnar said, was questionable, but he was impatient to have the gear in the water.

The nets are stored toward the front of the trawl deck on enormous reels the size of pickup trucks, in the same way you might wrap a ribbon around a spool of thread to keep it handy. Taj placed a hook into the aft end of the net from a winch that overhung the stern by fifteen feet, and Gunnar used controls in the wheelhouse to pull the pile of web and rope into the water. Taj then leaned over and retrieved the hook. As we steamed along at four knots Gunnar carefully let the force of the boat pull the quarter mile of net off the reel. What appeared to be an endless mass of twisted twine, rope and chain would enfold in the water to become a sophisticated shape resembling a giant funnel.

While the net paid out I kept an eye on the reel, watching for backlashes. You develop an eye for them, and an intuition as to how serious they are. If I raised my hand for an instant, Gunnar would stop and let me untangle the problem. Too many stops and you irritate the man in the wheelhouse, but you have to catch the tangles immediately.

If you don't, a simple three-strand backlash could turn into a nightmare where the net is wrapped around the spool in two directions. If you let that happen one too many times it's time to polish your resume.

Vidar's job was to watch the net as it sped by, making sure that everything light in the net would float upward in the water, and everything heavy would sink. In this way the net is free to open naturally.

There can be no links of chain caught in a mesh, no floats or hammerlocks wrapped around a breastline. He stood with his hands behind his back, smoking a cigarette, impassively watching.

The crew was split into two sides, each a mirror image of the other. Vidar and the combi worked the port side, Taj and I worked the starboard. We essentially made the same hookups, and after a few days, when the combi began to figure out what was going on, we would begin to compete.

When the net was in the water the cables began to stream off the spool. Gunnar was letting out the cables full bore now. With the net below the surface the boat was already less jumpy. Gunnar had the stern to the wind, and waves were lapping onto the deck, washing the thin sheet of ice away. Tomorrow we would have fish, and fire hoses to blow away the ice.

There were just two sets of hookups on this net: each side

had to connect a set of 3600 lb weights, then a set of cables, half as thick as a wrist and sixty feet long. These were attached to the "doors", -- massive rectangles of shaped steel that spread the net open as they were lowered into the water. The hooks alone on the cables weighed twenty pounds. The doors weighed three tons, and swung freely against the back of the boat. Heavy work, but mostly a matter of technique. There was a way to pick up a hook, a way to pull a cable without getting hurt, and it was the body that had to learn it, not the mind.

It is easy in this type of work to waste a lot of energy. Not too hard to get hurt, either. The trick is to watch out for the wire cables with the most slack, which sometimes behave in unpredictable ways.

Taj was good, and we were naturally finished long before Vidar. I watched Steve, the combi. I heard Tonni say that the kid had worked the oil rigs in the Gulf of Mexico. He was tall, well-built for the deck, not terribly clumsy. Beginners usually run around too much, waste a lot of energy, and get hurt. You move around too much and the odds naturally catch you quicker. But he wasn't doing much of that. His body seemed to be making the necessary adjustments, but his mind was clearly behind. That was natural. Everyone picked up the work at different speeds. Some never picked it up at all.

I've seen a hundred combis come up from the factory and can count on one hand the ones that have made it as far as deckhand.

By the time we had finished it was ten to two. No sign of the other shift. We had forgotten to give wake-up calls, but there would be no work until the first haul-back. I called them and we went in to eat.

I ate with Taj and Steve. Steve had been living on the streets of New Orleans following the oil bust a few years back. He was reluctant to speak about himself, but asked plenty of questions about his new job. I was tired, and left the two talking enthusiastically about door-legs, sweeps, cod-ends and gilson hooks.

On the way out I checked the posted list for Alani's cabin. It was two doors from mine. Alone in the hallway, I pressed an ear against her door. Silence. It was two-thirty. I hoped, for her sake, that she was sleeping soundly. She went to work at nine. I'd wake up in the middle of my shift at eight and bring her a dose of my tea.

Rusty was in the shower. I called through the bathroom door,

"Shot the net at one, Russ. Going to bed."

"Goodnight," I heard, over the shower. I would see him twelve hours later.

The bathroom was built off a small lounge that we shared with our neighbors. From the lounge, two doors led to two tiny cabins. Our cabin was just big enough for two bunks, a pair of thin closets, and a small bookshelf. Proust rested quietly in the middle of the shelf framed on either side by Rusty's string of Stephen Kings paperbacks.

I ran a finger down the spine of the first volume. Two trips before I had managed Ulysses. Twice, in fact. Second time with a guidebook to help me make sense of the obscure references, and language. That was a lonely and beautiful trip, in a strange way. I took my food directly from the line in the galley to the common lounge and ate alone every night, the old modern library edition of Ulysses spread out beside Tonni's many varieties of chicken.

Half the trip knee-deep in dying fish, half on the streets of Dublin, 1906. Tonight, however, I would simply sleep.

At eight I found Alani on the bow. She said she couldn't sleep, but that she was feeling a little better, out in the fresh air. The boat was heading straight into a stinging wind from the west. I wondered how someone from Hawaii could possible stand it. But she was telling me that she was from somewhere else.

"My mom is Polynesian. From the Marshall Islands. My Dad grew up in California but we moved to an island off the coast of Virginia when I was a baby. I grew up on islands all over the place but when I went to college it was in Bennington, Vermont. As far away from as the islands as I could get. Studied 'feminist theory' for awhile." She watched me carefully for a moment. "Had a couple of affairs with my professors but decided I didn't like women that way so much. Or missed men. Or something."

I shrugged. I thought of my ex-wife. My daughter. For me, now, they were like characters in a movie I had watched a few years back. A good movie, to be sure, and one that stays with you, but from a world away. "Life gets complex as you go on, it seems," I said. A white lie, I suppose, since I seem to have worked so very hard to simplify mine.

We talked for nearly an hour, warming to each other through the bitter weather, laughing about the turns and twists of our lives. Her father had been a commander in the Navy, and stole her mother away from a tiny island in the Marshalls twenty years before. They travelled like gypsies, it seemed, and always lived on small islands off various coasts – a lifestyle that her father appreciated but that her mother craved. The travel, I suppose, allowed her to develop an apparent ease with people, but I detected a nonchalance, a distance that might have been mistaken for coldness. Not by me, though. I found that languor as attractive as the rest of her – it was an island ease, and one that I recognized from my time in the Caribbean. It fit, somehow, perfectly with the setting, as we looked out on a coal-black sea broken here and there with white wisps of wave blown up by a bitter wind.

She herself marveled about the quirks of fate that lead her to a place like the Bering Sea in the middle of January. There was a hint of light on the horizon, but there would be no sun for another two hours, and then for only a short while.

"I meant to say how much I appreciated the tea ... and the touch last night. I mean when you put your hand on my neck. It was – I mean I felt better."

She looked up at me. I could see her face better now in the dusky light.

We are animals, after all. As sure as I was standing there, alive and breathing on a steel deck in an inhumanly cold sea, I wanted to touch her again. For a second I felt no wind whatsoever. I reached out and brushed aside a lock of hair that was pressed against her cheek.

"It's almost daylight," I said. "We'll get you some more tea."

That night she would come to my cabin, or I would go to hers. That is how it happens. Intimacy comes quickly on the boats, or it doesn't come at all. For the women, who are outnumbered five to one, it's a constant pressure to choose, and the choices are usually made within the first week at sea. For the men, or those of us who really lived out there at sea, and not just visited, the first week was spent in a sharp hunt for opportunity. This is not something we planned. It was visceral, animalistic, probably hormone-driven. The mating cycle, compressed.

The entire processing crew were assembled in the mess room, having been summoned by the captain for an introductory greeting, a pep talk, and a safety meeting. Eighty percent of the processors had heard the same extended speech at least half a dozen times, and the meeting was aimed mainly at the newcomers, but attendance, at least for the processors, was mandatory. I was surprised to see the Japanese contingent, a group of ten or so young men who were surimi experts. Having little or no understanding of English, they rarely attended these meetings. They occupied their own table, and chatted amiably among themselves.

As for myself, I had suffered through various forms of the same speech by different captains for years, so I wasn't about to sit through this one. Actually, Jon was entertaining. In fact, I often thought he had missed his calling as a stand-up comedian, but it was my immediate goal to prepare Alani's medicinal concoction and return to bed. Jon had yet to make his appearance, and the processors were getting fidgety.

I was working with the mixture near the door of the galley when I heard Tonni's distinct voice carrying through the galley.

"But how can you let them *do*" it?"

"Do what, Tonni?" Jon was speaking.

"You know, let them treat you that way? For God's sake, show the bastards who's the boss. Exercise some authority... *something*"."

Jon responded but I couldn't make out the words. I had overheard something that was none of my business anyway. I heard the voices approaching and I finished my task and slipped out of the mess room. Jon would be wounded if I walked out on his speech. As far I was concerned, I should be asleep.

Alani was in her cabin. It was five minutes to nine. I handed her the lukewarm tea.

"Thanks, Fish. But you know, I barely need it. I feel so much better." She downed the drink in a few big gulps. Smiled.

I said, "That'll just settle the matter once and for all, then. Since we put a net in the water, the boat has calmed down a lot, anyway."

"I'll say." She looked at her watch. "I have to go."

"Yes, you do. Should be a good show in the mess room. Jon's a crack-up."

"Cute, too, in a little-boy way." She winked. Touched her tongue to her upper lip in a way that gave me a shiver.

"I suppose," I said quietly.

She took my head and drew me in. Planted a nice kiss on my lips and said, "You're a doll. Thanks again. I gotta go to work."

"Go, already."

I let myself out and headed back toward the cabin. On my way I glanced out to the trawl deck. No sign of a haul-back. Not the best news.

But just as I was pulling the covers up to my chin I heard the winches start up. As I drifted off I was thinking about fish, thousands of them. Fish, and Alani's petite figure racing up the narrow stairs.

The bag of fish, Rusty was telling me, was pulled up at about nine-thirty.

"I heard the winches," I said.

"Was kind of a joke. Six hours pulling the biggest net we got -

- hell, the biggest net in the world, the bag was maybe a third full. I think they wrote it up as thirty tons."

"Who was fishing?"

"Um, Martin fished the net for six hours, but Gunnar stepped up at nine to do the haul-back. Martin's gonna work two-to-eight, I guess. Gunnar, eight-to-two."

"Six on, six off for those guys, huh?"

Rusty nodded. "Yup. I hope the deck crew stays with twelve's."

"We'll stay. None of us want to work sixes. Least of all, Vidar."

Rusty stood up to go. It was two-fifteen in the afternoon. Brightest time of the day. I followed him halfway to the galley, just to get some air.

I said, "Thirty tons, huh?"

He turned at the door. "Yeah, but it's not so bad because no one else caught anything. I think the Emerald Sea posted fifteen. They were fishing maybe a quarter-mile away."

He waved and stepped inside. I could hear the distant, rhythmic whine of filet machines in the factory. Behind us a sea of a million gulls sitting in our wake, feeding on the scraps that trailed from the waste chutes in the factory, stretched to the horizon. Thousands of others flew in an endless circle around the boat, sometimes landing to scoop up a piece of fishgut, a chunk of rejected surimi, anything remotely edible.

Thirty tons was a disappointment. The factory could handle a thousand tons of pollock a day. From that they could produce about a hundred tons of surimi, maybe thirty tons of roe. Surimi is the inert, white end-product made from fish fillets that is used to create fake crab and other inventive delicacies. For this the boats receive about a dollar a pound from the Japanese, but roe can bring many times that. It is the eggs, the roe, during the short mating season of the pollock, that bring the real money to the factory fleet.

For the Duchess to reach maximum production, the fishmaster and mate must supply the boat with a hundred-ton bag of fish every few hours, around the clock. For this they are paid about a hundred-fifty and a hundred thousand dollars a year, respectively. But the pressure is enormous, especially because the dwindling resource has gradually, over the past few years, reduced the fishing season from twelve months a year to about four. Four months to make forty million dollars.

With such high stakes, every moment counts, every haul-back is critical. Thirty-ton bags in the middle of roe season are not acceptable.

The winches started and I looked up to see Martin behind the control panel. He waved. Signaled to get ready for a haul-back. I checked my watch. Two-thirty. Taj appeared at the door of the deck shack.

"I'll get Steve," I shouted.

As I descended the stairs to the factory the din grew louder. I stuck my head through the door of the upper-level and covered my ears. The processors were going through the thirty tons from that morning. The Japanese must have aged the fish five hours or so, hoping for the highest quality surimi.

The six fillet machines stretched out before me in a row. A pair of operators, each with music headphones strapped to their heads, stood working before them.

I watched the couple at the first machine for a moment, mildly interested. This was my job for a year. On another boat, ages ago, it seemed.

The operators were a man and a woman. I remembered they were married, from a tiny farm town in Montana. They'd been coming up regularly for years. They were experts. She chewed tobacco. Kept an empty coffee can by her feet which she used as a spittoon. He stood on her left, throwing fish from a conveyor before him onto a slotted belt that fed the machine endlessly. One fish per slot, all facing the same direction. He didn't miss a slot. She straightened the fish as they went by, tucking their tails under a steel bar, aligning their heads, occasionally leaning into the machine among the rotating knives to clear them of debris. They fed the machine continually, effortlessly, at a hundred-twenty fish per minute, seven thousand an hour, for six straight hours. Then they went to bed for six, while a pair of replacements took over. Then they returned.

If the boat remained supplied with fish, the couple from

Montana would continue in this way for three weeks until the thousand-ton freezer hold was filled. Then it was back to Dutch for thirty hours, then back to sea. They signed sixty-day contracts. Ten days after each successful three-week trip the office would send their bank two checks, each for about ten thousand dollars. After their two-month contract ended in late March, they would return to their tiny farm town in Montana, maybe sixty thousand dollars richer. They probably made twice as much as the mayor.

Steve was nowhere to be seen. I was not surprised; being brand new, he couldn't know how to operate a fillet machine. I checked downstairs and a Japanese technician pointed to a ladder that led to the sugar room. Steve was breaking open fifty-pound bags of sugar additive and pouring them into a wide hopper. He wore a dust mask, which was a good thing, for I could hardly see him through the white cloud that rose around the hopper. He was tossing the empty bags in a another hopper that was a quarter-full of sugar.

"What's this?" I pointed to the second hopper.

"Junk sugar," he said through the mask. "I'm supposed to check every bag. If there's lumps, I dump it into that one. Not too many, so far."

"We're hauling back," I said.

The sugar room was hot. He was sweating as he pulled off the mask. "Thanks, man. I'm sick of this."

I headed toward a tunnel created among the stacks of sugar

bags.

"Shortcut," I said. "Vidar made this. It leads straight to the deck shack. He comes in here to sleep."

"It's warm enough."

"And quiet as hell. I can't hear the factory, and I don't hear the winches outside. Amazing."

We crawled through the tunnel. He said, "First haul-back of my career."

"Piece of cake," I said. "Just take it easy. It's basically everything we did last night, but reversed."

"I don't even remember what we did last night. It's all a bunch of goddamned wires and rope to me."

We put our suits on in the deck shack. I saw Vidar and Taj standing on the trawl deck, waiting for the doors to come up.

"Takes time," I said. "There's a lot to this. When I was a carpenter I started reading blueprints after about three months. Here, it took me two years to figure out a net plan."

"I don't even want to know what a net plan is."

"Just a blueprint for a net. In three dimensions, though. You have to imagine the third dimension."

"Like I said, I don't wanna know about it. Just tell me what cable to pull and when."

"You got the right attitude," I said.

The main-wires shook as the pair of doors slammed into the back of the boat. Martin heaved on the two huge winches, pinning the doors tight against the stern so we could lean out and unhook them. A tricky part of the operation. If you're not careful you can get an arm caught between the six-thousand pound door and the stern. Then you lay in your bunk on morphine for three days until someone can skiff you to a boat that happens to be returning to Dutch Harbor.

The doorlegs are the next bit of fun. Steel cables, sixty-feet long, as thick as a cucumber. They need to be removed from the cables that are attached to the net. There are a dozen ways to do this efficiently. I like to pick them up high in the air with a hook dropped from straight above. My partner leans over the railing and grabs them. I unhook them as they are lowered, he pulls them onto the deck. Done well, it looks like an exotic Olympic sport.

Instinctively, I glanced upward two stories at the wheelhouse, checking out the audience. Gunnar stood apprehensively beside the control panel. Martin was doing the haul-back, but Gunnar had fished the net previous six hours. It was his bag of pollock.

Jon stood on the other side, watching both the action on deck, and Martin on the controls. I admired his strong curiosity about a process from which he would likely be forever excluded.

Tonni appeared briefly at Jon's side, ghostlike, in an enormous galley apron. Hastings, of all people, sat in a chair pulled close to a window on the far side of the wheelhouse. He was calmly smoking a pipe. Nowhere did I see the shape for which I searched for most, then Alani appeared, for a moment, in the doorway leading to the galley. She smiled and waved, held up a plate of snacks. She left them by the door.

The net by now was halfway on the reel, halfway stretching into the sea behind us. Gunnar pointed a pair of binoculars behind the boat. The sea was fairly calm. At this point if there was a full bag of fish it would rise up a hundred yards behind as like a surfacing whale. There was nothing. Not even as the last quarter of the net spun onto the spool. A very bad sign, indeed.

When the bag reached the end of the stern ramp, Martin sent down the huge gilson hook. I slapped a thick rope from the bag onto the hook and he heaved it onto the deck. It was nearly empty. I saw Gunnar throw the binoculars to the floor and move away from the window. Only Martin was left, then he too, disappeared. No word on whether to shoot the net.

I motioned for Taj to open a hatch in the deck that led to a tank in the factory. I reached for the zipper line to open the bag. Vidar held up a hand. "Forget it. It's just a ton. We'll shoot it out again."

Then Gunnar appeared and spoke in Norwegian over the loudspeaker. Vidar shook his head angrily. Gunnar raised his voice. Vidar cursed in his native language and scrambled up to the wheelhouse. He appeared ten minutes later, angry.

"We don't need a another net," he said, "We need another fishmaster."

"What's up?" I asked.

"We have to go through the net. Fix every hole."

"There are no holes."

"I know that. But try to convince Gunnar. He knows there are no holes. He says if we find none, we must change the net."

"Go through the net, then change it? The whole thing'll take a shift, maybe more."

Vidar shrugged. "Just get it ready."

It would take four of us hours to pull the quarter-mile long net off the reel in sixty-foot bites, pulling through each section, looking for holes. Each mesh was anywhere from four to twenty-five feet long, composed of twine as thick as a little finger. If there were holes, they might be a hundred feet across. But holes that size we would have surely seen during the haul-back.

Vidar explained the extent of the disaster: both the Ocean Rover and the Pacific Orion, fishing on either side of us, had caught a hundred tons each. It was inconceivable that we should have missed the fish. If anyone in the office bothered to study the fishing reports, they would see what happened immediately. Gunnar was grasping at straws in order to save face.

Ten hours later we were finished with the net, had found no holes of significance, and were ready to spool down the cables. There were four, each two hundred meters long. We needed a fifth person to run the winch, and Tonni appeared at the right moment.

"I heard you boys have some salt. I'm pickling some delicious redfish from the factory. Can you spare some?"

I said, "Trade you fifty pounds, Tonni, for fifteen minutes of your time. Just grab that winch handle, there, yep, and pull."

But after five minutes we ran into problems. Backlashed wire, twists, and kinks. It would be at least an hour. I told Steve to get Tonni a bag of salt from the sugar room. Vidar tied a piece of rope to the winch handle in such a way as to operate it with a foot. Tonni took the bag of sugar and glanced at the winch contraption.

"You boys are clever."

"Just save us some fish," I said.

By two A.M. there was a new net on the reel. The other shift had arrived. Vidar and Bjorn, his counterpart, spoke quietly in Norwegian. I told Rusty what had happened.

"You guys'll shoot this net any minute, now. God help you if he can't catch anything with it."

He looked at his watch. "Martin's on now. We'll catch something."

"Hope so."

Twelve hours on a steel deck in January in the Bering Sea. I had never enjoyed a hot shower as much in my life. Afterward, I opened the door to find Alani stretched out on the couch in the our lounge like a native angel in a Gauguin painting.

"You wouldn't believe how happy I am to see you," I said.

She smiled. "I believe it. Come over here."

I obeyed. She was a skilled, enthusiastic lover. Sex at sea is unlike anywhere else. Something about the minimalism, the endless motion of the boat, magnifies the tactile sense. Long after we had made love for hours we lay entwined, whispering. I traced slow arcs across her belly, marveling at the impossible smoothness, the subtle rise toward her pubis. I fell asleep with my head between her breasts, gauging her heartbeat against the rocking of the ship.

I wish I could say the fishing improved. Even now, after everything that has happened, it would be hard to explain those first few days.

Fish are mysterious creatures. Jung felt they symbolize the elements of the unconscious mind. Throw a net into the water, you are delving beneath the surface of your psyche. I have no trouble with that point of view.

As Gunnar pulled up one empty bag after another, he began to deteriorate. Martin was fishing a little better, but not much. The afternoon of the third day Vidar came down from the wheelhouse looking grave. Gunnar was going through half a bottle of stomach pills in a shift. He was not sleeping. His eyes were swollen from staring at the fish-finding video screen. He had given up talking to the other fishmasters of the fleet. Vidar felt that the radio silence was conclusive evidence that the man was finished professionally.

Yet there was no pity forthcoming from Vidar; the bosun

continued to rage against the tired old captain. Haulbacks were turning into a war of wills between the deck and the wheelhouse. During one such battle, Gunnar illustrated his point by using the controls to yank a thick cable from Vidar's hand. The bosun responded by pitching a half-pound shackle through the lower window of the wheelhouse, missing Hastings in his chair by a fraction of an inch. The engineer ceased that day to be a member of our audience. On the fourth day the production reports came in from the surrounding boats. Every boat had packed at least three hundred tons of finished product. The Duchess had frozen sixty. After that no one appeared at the wheelhouse windows to watch haulbacks except the American captain, Jon.

The dread crept down from the bridge and infected the entire crew. The first wave of processors quit. Newcomers, mostly. Eight or so. They refused to leave their cabins, except to eat. They demanded to be skiffed off to a boat heading for Dutch Harbor, where they could sign with any productive ship that came along. I was shocked to hear Taj talk of leaving.

We were sitting at the table in the deck shack. Vidar was sleeping in the sugar room. He slept now more than ever, it seemed.

Taj was saying, "No problem for you to sit there, Fish, and tell me not to worry 'bout the money. Don't matter if this boat sinks to the bottom, you makin' three hundred a day. Look at me. Day 'fore yesterday, two processors worked one machine twelve hours. Rest of the poor fools sprayed down the factory with hoses. Know what I made? Twenty-seven dollars, brutha, twenty-seven."

I took the empty cup from his hand and filled it. I handed it to him and said, "Hey, I know it's bad. I've been through luck worse than this. But the only reason I'm guaranteed money now is because I stuck it out through the worst of times."

He took sip of coffee and made a face. "Yeah Fish, but you know it sucks to get up every morning lookin' at twelve hours, knowin' you aunt gettin' paid."

I stared at my partner. "Taj, will you answer me one question? Just one question."

"Yeah."

"Why are you here? Why are you fishing? Is it just for the money? 'Cause if it is, I have no sympathy. You want big money quick, you rob a bank."

The island man leaned closer and narrowed his eyes. A rare moment when he wasn't aloof. He said, "Fish, I *like* this. I really do. Maybe I'm no fanatic like you, but I have fun out here. But I'm a deckhand on this boat so I can save some money, go to school. I got plans for my life." He looked around the room. "And the rest of it ain't gonna be lived here."

"Good for you," I answered. "Plans. I hope they come to pass. No ... I'm serious. I really do. But what I'm talking about has nothing to do with fishing. Or plans. I'm talking about the here and now. I'm talking about putting everything you have into the moment as it comes along."

"Shit, " he stretched out the word, "Hard to put somethin' in a moment ain't worth two dollars, Fish."

I sighed. How many times had I had this conversation, and with how many people? I said, "Okay, you wanna talk about plans. Well plans don't happen without some commitment. You know, the idea of finishing something you start no matter what happens?"

"Fish, brutha, you sound like a fuckin' guidance counselor."

I tossed my empty paper cup into the garbage and stood up. "And you sound like a spoiled high school kid who doesn't want to wake up in the morning.

I wanted to find Alani for a little positive reassurance, but she found me first. We met in the raingear room. She was upset.

"What is it?"

"It's Tonni. The housekeeper quit and won't come out of her cabin. Now I'm housekeeping. Tonni's handling the galley alone."

"Good for him," I said.

"Not for us, though."

"What do you mean?"

"Fish, Monique worked from two in the morning to two in the afternoon. The exact opposite of your shift. I'll never see you." She was right, of course. People that work at sea on opposite, 12-hour shifts might as well work three thousand miles away. It's possible to live on a 280-foot boat for three months and never see or even meet half the people that work with you.

Until that moment I had stood outside what I thought was a fleeting and overblown crisis. Bad days, even bad weeks come and go in the fishing industry. Before I received the contract that guaranteed me a wage of $374 each day, seven days a week, I had sometimes worked for a hundred hours in a noisy, slime-filled factory for ten cents an hour. But I never thought about the money, not for a minute. I was one of those who came to Alaska because I was steamrolled by the general insanity of the lower forty-eight, and well, for a lot of internal reasons that I will someday, somehow sort out.

And so, I threw myself into every little task with an enthusiasm, a boundless energy, perhaps even an unbalanced ability to focus. I was graciously rewarded for my attitude with choice posts and promotions, and had only that year begun to calm down and take things a little more easily. Things like Alani's affection, for instance.

Now the petty greed, the impatience of the whining "I want it NOW" crowd had somehow snuck in and stolen a large part of my ability to enjoy the day. I was beginning to lose my temper.

"Where's Tonni?"

She turned my wrist to look at my watch. Midnight.

"Asleep, probably."

I kissed her forehead and stepped past her. She grabbed my sleeve. "Fish, don't wake him up for this. It's no big deal."

"It is a big deal. To me, anyway."

"Fish, he's my boss."

I took a few breaths, cooled myself down a little. I pulled her close, put on my most rational face. "Sweetheart, Tonni and I will have a very mature conversation. Just like a couple of grownups. I've been at this for years, and I haven't made a true enemy yet. Trust me."

This drew a wry smile from her. She pushed me lightly away.

"Go, then. Save the day."

It may not seem like much, but on a boat in the middle of the Bering Sea in the winter, whether you get to sleep with the person you want to is about as important as it gets.

I climbed to the fifth level. The steward lived a floor below the wheelhouse, on the same deck as the other officers.

Tonni was standing in the middle of his cabin, taking up most of the floor space. He was dressed in immaculate white with a floppy chef's hat covering his melon-shaped head. His fat lips looked more crimson than usual against the sweaty pallor of his skin, then I realized he was wearing a light coating of makeup. The paleness made his tiny black eyes recede even further into the folds of his face. He held a pair of scissors lightly in one hand and a spray bottle in the other, and was positioned in a sort of awkward embrace around a man seated in a chair in the middle of the room. He was cutting the captain's hair.

Tonni's mouth made a perfect O when I stepped through the

open door. "What an absolute surprise! To what do we owe such honor?"

"I didn't know you were a barber," I said.

"Son, you surprise me. I am *hardly* a barber. I am an *artiste*. Isn't that right, captain?"

Jon swiveled slightly beneath the towel wrapped around his neck. "I'd feel better if you were a barber," he said.

If the captain was suffering from the tension throughout the ship he was showing none of it. In fact he seemed to have developed a certain glow, and with it, a bit of presence.

For the past three days I had stayed away from the wheelhouse. But I was curious. "How's Gunnar been, Jon?"

The captain frowned. He tried to turn my way but Tonni held his head firmly and clipped at his left sideburn.

"Not good. Sick, I think. He's been having stomach cramps every night. Tonight he left early. He called Martin up at eleven. Then he went to bed."

"Nerves," stated Tonni.

Jon shrugged. "The office is calling, faxing every day. They want to know what the hell is going on. I wouldn't want to have to answer that phone."

Tonni scowled. "Fish, did you come all the way up here just to bother us with this crap?"

"Not exactly."

The big man suddenly showed me his teeth. "Well, I'm very

glad you did come, because I have a favor to ask you."

"Oh?" Such a happy coincidence, I was thinking.

Tonni spoke slowly as he concentrated on Jon's hair. "I need to get to those ten pallets of food stored in the lower freezer."

"How much you need?"

"Oh ... all of it. I mean, if that's not too difficult."

I thought about it. "I suppose we can open up all the hatches up front. Crane the pallets onto the bow. Close up the hatches, hand it down to you. It'll take half the shift."

"Well, I thought since there's been such poor fishing we could take advantage of our ... misfortune."

"Okay. When?"

"Um, tomorrow, after dinner sometime?"

"Consider it done. We'll need your help, of course."

"Of course, Fish."

"And, uh, I'll need your help on something else."

Tonni cocked an eyebrow. Waited. He was busy wrapping the captain's face with a large steamy towel.

"I understand Alani's the new housekeeper."

Tonni pulled a long red frown across the expanse of his face. "She is. That awful bitch, what's her name, Monique, she quit on me. Won't come out of her cabin until she gets a ride to Dutch."

Jon spoke through the towel. "She'll starve to death. We're not going to Dutch Harbor until this boat is full or our fuel tanks are empty."

Tonni said, "Let her starve. She's anorexic anyway." He pursed his lips. "Furthermore, I understand there are other reasons for Queen Monique to remain in her chamber." He cast a meaningful look in my direction.

I tried to picture the housekeeper, but to tell the truth I hadn't paid too much attention to her. I remembered a tall wispy girl with black hair, pale complexion. Exceptionally pretty, but very quiet. But I didn't care about boat gossip just now, and told I the steward as much.

"There are times," the Tonni answered, "when a boy needs to listen to gossip."

I let that one pass. I was letting the strange man lead me off track. His moon-sized mask leered at me across the top of the captain's head. Reminded me of the face of the beluga whales that cavort at the mouth of the Kenai river in October.

I said, "Look, I'm not going to pretend you don't know about Alani and me, and I think you know the hours I work. So I'd appreciate a little flexibility here."

The grin evaporated. "Oh, I see," he said. "And so the Northern Duchess should rearrange its work schedules to suit your sexual appetite?"

I was used to Tonni. I felt I knew him pretty well. It was a matter of working your way around an ego twice the size of Kodiak Island. Besides, he was only showing off in front of the captain, who remained impassive under the hot towels.

"I might not have put it that way, Tonni, but you can figure it any way you need to. I can't believe there has to be a set time to do the laundry, clean the walls. Just asking for a little break here."

Tonni removed the towels and gently applied shaving creme to Jon's face. Then he pulled a long straight razor from a case and began the shave. He was a pro with the razor, but he didn't say a word for six minutes. When he finished, he wiped the captain's face with a damp cloth and rubbed in after-shave lotion. He handed Jon a mirror. There wasn't a trace of good will when he turned to me.

"I like you, Fish. I always have. You're intelligent. About most things. I just have a tendency to protect those I respect, that's all."

"From what? False intimacy? AIDS? What business of it is yours, anyway?"

"I just don't want to see you get hurt, that's all."

"Bullshit, Tonni. Let me worry about myself, you worry about yourself. Very simple." I looked at the captain for some support, but he was examining the condition of his cuticles.

Tonni took a small step backward. Held up his hands. A gesture of expanse, generosity. The moment we had worked toward had arrived.

"Fish, you tell Alani she can work any hours she damn well pleases. And you take care of yourself."

"Thank you, Tonni." I stifled an impulse to bow as I backed

from the room.

It was time for a dose of sanity. With Jon occupied and Gunnar in bed, I knew Martin would be alone in the wheelhouse. I was hoping for some perspective regarding the string of bad luck that threatened to rip to shreds the social fabric of the boat.

He sat in the far swivel chair staring pensively at the fish-finding monitor. He greeted me with a grunt and returned his gaze to the screen. Martin looked terrible. His hair was unkempt, his clothes disheveled. It looked like he hadn't been to bed for three days. I took the chair across from the helm.

"I hear Gunnar is sick," I said.

He yawned. "Gunnar is lost," he said. "Lost and stubborn. The worst kind of combination."

"But there must be something else if--"

"There is. Look at this."

He pointed to the screen. A side-view representation of the sloping ocean bottom barely moved across a light blue field. Above, at different levels, were pockets of red and orange flecks. Fish.

He said, "The blue, as you know, is the water column. Right now ... " he trailed a finger across to the side of the screen to a number,

"... five hundred fathoms. Deep water. And the fish are at four hundred here ... three hundred here ... maybe three fifty here. All over the place, right?"

"Got it."

"Now look at this screen."

It was a digitized readout of the depth of the net, as calculated by the ship's computer, based on a signal received by a sonar unit.

"The net is at three-fifty. I need to move it to two-fifty. No problem, because the computer has done the work. It tells me here," pointing to a smaller readout, "how much cable to reel in. I type in this number, press this button, and off we go."

We watched the main winches on the trawl deck begin to spin, heaving in cable at full speed. Taj stepped out onto the deck and looked up at the darkened wheelhouse, hoping, perhaps, for a haulback. He shielded his eyes against the halogen lights, but I knew he couldn't see into the bridge.

Martin took the microphone. His voice, tired and discouraged, carried across the deck.

"Back to your nap, Taj. Just hauling in some cable."

I looked at the screen. As the depth of the net approached two-hundred fifty fathoms, I heard the winches slow, then stop.

Martin pointed to a small red cluster of dots at the two-fifty mark. "In ten minutes we will catch these fish."

"So what's the problem?"

"The problem is, there will be no fish in the net. I *know* this, I can feel it. And I've been right almost every time this trip."

"But how can that be?"

Martin dismissed the screen with a wave. "Fishing isn't a Nintendo game. Those are red dots on a screen. That's all they really are. The technology works most of the time, but sometimes it fails. Gunnar should know this better than anyone, but somewhere along the line he's forgotten it. Now it's all he has, and he clings to it. The only time I can catch anything is when he's not hanging on my shoulder."

"But what do you do that he doesn't?"

He shook his head impatiently. " I can't explain it. Sometimes you have to know when to pull up and leave an area. Go a few miles away. You have to have a feeling for whether the screen is telling you the truth. If it were up to me, we'd leave the whole fleet, find our own place to fish. He'll never do that."

I looked again at the video. "So you're saying the sonar is screwed up?"

The fishmate frowned at the screen. "No. I've calibrated it a hundred times this trip. If there's something wrong, it's in the software, but I don't see how that could be. Everything else works fine. He shook his head slowly.

"No ... what I'm saying is that Gunnar is screwed up. He's the fishmaster, he's running the show. He's good, damned good."

He looked at me. "Maybe you don't believe that. But in Norway he was one of the best. He waited like a hawk for this job. When Oddbjorn Huse left last month, Gunnar called in every favor he had to get on. I think he wants to finish his career here on the Duchess, maybe even try to break Huse's world record.

"But we've lost four days already. That's maybe two million dollars. It's almost impossible to catch up after a start like that. Gunnar has made himself sick over it."

There was nothing for me to say. It all came back to Gunnar, who was collapsing from the responsibility he had imposed upon himself and the pressure from the office. I moved to the front windows and put a hand on the cool glass. The wind shifted and began to blow the tops of the nearest waves onto our bow. I listened to the wind whip through the patched hole that Vidar had smashed the day before. The boat rose and fell indifferently beneath us.

Behind me, I heard Martin say, "The fish will come back. They always do. The goal is to not kill ourselves worrying about it."

But judging from the look on his face he was in no position to live by that advice.

I rarely wake up in a bad mood, but sometimes it happens, and then what are you going to do? Just roll with it. Maybe it had something to do with the fact that I woke up alone. Alani didn't appear the night before and I didn't want to push it by chasing her down. I knew enough to give her what everyone needed at some point, especially here -- privacy.

But I'm sure it was my mood that caused me to start wrong with Hastings that afternoon. For all I knew he came back to apologize for the bananas, but I never gave him the chance. First thing I said to him when I found him sitting in our deck shack reading a magazine was,

"Waiting for us to break something?"

He sneered. Happy for the opportunity to duel. "I received a fax today, Fish. The office suggests I weld some bars on this door. That way we can let you guys out for haulbacks, put you back in before you touch anything."

I looked around for Taj. The coffee pot was gone, so I figured he went for a refill. Vidar was probably napping again.

"Look at it this way, Hastings. There has to be some balance in the world. Think of Yin and Yang. We break, you fix. What would you do without us?"

"I can think of a lot of things."

I was tired of this already, but he wasn't ready to quit. He threw the magazine on the table.

"Do me a favor, Fish, and keep your bimbo out of my control room."

I let the words sink in, do their work inside me. I stared at him, mustering every ounce of will to keep from reaching across the table and pinning his scrawny neck to the wall.

He must have seen something in my face. He said, "Hey ... easy, Fish. I didn't think you cared about her so much."

"Hastings, they teach you any social skills at all at MIT?"

He ignored that.and said, "Look, she came down to clean. She's new at the job, I understand that. I politely told her that I would take care of the cleaning. She insisted that she wouldn't mind 'straightening up' about once a week. She's strong-willed, all right.

"But the last thing I need is a ... young lady with a feather duster molling around the equipment." He cleared his throat. His manner had suddenly softened. "I thought if you could explain to her ..."

I had no problem with that. I couldn't see Alani wanting to be around the likes of Hastings under any circumstances. Yet I was suddenly curious why he was so protective of his control room.

But he had other things to say. "Look, Fish, let's give this confrontational garbage a rest. You're probably as tired of it as I am. Engineers and deckhands were never made to get along, but there's no reason we have to be at each other's throats. We should be sticking together anyway."

"We?"

"I mean we Americans. If you haven't noticed, the Norwegians have been having a bit of trouble lately. I think their 'advising' days are coming to an end. I wouldn't cling to them too tightly."

"Hastings, I don't 'cling' to anyone. But you know as well as I do that some of these guys are the best fishermen you'll ever see. I've learned more in three years of watching Vidar than I could in ten years in any American academy."

"Vidar, huh? I understand Vidar is starting to hit the sauce again. He's been in and out of clinics, Fish. I'd watch him if I were you."

"Fuck off, Hastings."

He shrugged. He stood up and looked out onto the trawl deck. "Suit yourself. It's not my ass out there on the line every day."

I waited for him to leave. What he said about Vidar bothered me. And where the hell was Taj?

I crawled through the tunnel in the sugar room and found Vidar fast asleep in a hidden nest he had made among the bags of sugar. His body lay twisted unnaturally, and his head was thrown back. I could hear a steady, light snore. Behind him was an open can of soda. I stuck a finger into the opening and licked it. A slimy mixture of what tasted faintly like grain alcohol and coca-cola.

In one sense it was none of my business. I had heard plenty about Vidar's problems. That he hadn't been to see his family in Norway in three years, that he sometimes collapsed in elevators in Seattle, shaking and screaming with the DT's. And, as Hastings reminded me, that he had checked into treatment centers.

But I had never known him to drink on the boat. It was fishing, I believed, that had kept him alive thus far. I couldn't believe he was giving up his only haven of sobriety.

But he was drunk. No question about it. Fortunately there had been very little to do, but if the fishing improved, he would have to perform. For now he could sleep it off.

When I crawled back into the deck shack, Taj was dumping a bucket of fresh coffee into our pot. "Where you been?" I asked. I tried not to show my irritation but we had worked together for a month now. He knew me.

"I had to make this coffee myself. And I brought cakes. What do you mean, where've I been? What's the matter with you lately, Fish?"

I moved to the doorway, looked out at the water. "Sorry, Taj. Things have been a little ... screwed up."

"You talking about Alani?"

"What about Alani?" I recalled the cryptic hints from Tonni the night before.

"Nothin about Alani. I thought maybe you two were having problems. Just forget it."

"It's okay. Everything is okay with Alani and me. There're some other things ... tell you what. How about you go into the workshop, take the grinder, and cut some steel pipe. Do it right under the fire alarm."

Taj looked at me. "You losing it, Fish? Is everyone losing it around here?"

"Just do it. If anyone asks, you're going to use the pipe as a cheater bar for the shackle wrench. Or something. I don't care what you say, just set off the alarm. Use those coated pipes in the corner. They'll smoke like hell. I'll be back up here after it's over."

I didn't give him time for more questions. I took the stairs past the two factory levels. I noticed Steve was being trained at the first machine by the couple from Montana. He was spending most of his time in the factory now, since we so rarely hauled back the net.

Inside the lower factory level I saw some Japanese technicians in the distance, hovering over their esoteric equipment, otherwise it was quiet. I slipped through a hatch that led to the engine room without anyone noticing.

The two huge Wartsilla engines were running full bore in the engine pit below. Just above and off to the side of the port engine I found a place to crouch behind a tall tool cabinet. From my hiding place I could look over the tops of the engines and into the glass-enclosed control room. Hastings sat at his computer with his ear protectors draped around his neck. The noise from the engines was deafening. I pressed my hands to my ears and waited for the fire alarm.

When it went off he fairly leapt from his seat. I saw him run to a panel where he pushed a flashing red button. A digital readout appeared that read "TRAWL WORKSHOP". He cursed and stabbed the button again. The readout went black. Then he placed the ear protectors on and left the control room. He passed three feet from me on the way out. Angry as ever. Taj would have to deal with him.

I wasted no time. The control room was a mess. I could see why Alani had offered to clean it. Empty coffee cups were flung about the room, various technical manuals lay open, haphazardly strewn across the floor. On the far wall was the main control panel for the ship. Across from that was a long desk that held a computer, a printer, and the new fax machine, which rested on a new shelf Hastings had built onto the desk.

I wasn't sure what I was looking for, but I thought the fax machine might be a good place to start. In a drawer in the desk I found a thin folder labeled "fax file". Starting with the first day in

January there was a record of every fax sent and by Hastings' machine. There weren't many. Mostly it was technical questions and answers to other boats, a few faxes to the office requesting parts for various items. I was disappointed. Then I noticed a small garbage can beneath the fax machine. It was half-filled with wadded papers. I reached to the bottom and opened one. It was the original of a fax that I didn't see in the file. It read:

To: Larry Marino, Operations Manager,　　Northern Seafood's
From: Gordon Hastings, Chief Engineer, Northern Duchess
Date: January 14, 1993
RE: Recent production reports for the Northern Duchess

Larry: I feel compelled to report a grave situation on the Duchess that I can no longer ignore. Please understand it is with the best interests of the company that I furnish you with the following information, which I have obtained from my own sources:

"Vessel"	"Date/Time"	Catch (tons)
Aurora Sea	1/7/93-0600	85.0
Bering Victor	1/7/93-0730	105.0
Saga Clipper	1/7/93-0500	75.0
Northern Duchess	1/7/93-0630	11.0
Golden Phoenix	1/8/93-1100	120.0
Saga Clipper	1/8/93-1130	95.0
Northern Duchess	1/8/93-1100	5.0

This is a sample. I believe it effectively illustrates my point, which is that there is something quite wrong with the performance of our current fishmaster. You and I have always had a rapport, Larry, and I hope you will understand this fax for what it is. I have no ill will for Mr. Eriksen, I wish merely to provide you with an outside and perhaps more objective point of view than that which you may receive from the bridge of the Northern Duchess.

Thanks, Larry. See you in Seattle.

I had barely finished reading when I heard the hatch close from the lower factory level. I grabbed the plastic garbage bag from the can and sprinted out of the control room. I made it to the tool cabinet just before Hastings made his appearance. He passed by, stopping to check fluid levels before returning to the control room. When I saw his thin back hunched over the computer keyboard I slipped up the stairs and onto the trawl deck.

Taj was gone. I saw it was dinnertime. I had a date with Alani to eat that night in the cabin lounge, but I quickly went through the rest of the garbage from the control room. Only two more items of significance. One was another letter to the operations manager adding more catch data but also unabashedly providing a list of some of his former classmates from the marine academy. There was also a terse but sympathetic reply from Larry Marino essentially telling Hastings to mind his own business.

As I stood on line in the mess room I saw Taj giving the evil eye from a table near the door. He must have gotten a royal chewing from Hastings. I signaled an apology and got him to understand that I'd explain later. He shrugged. Grinned. Happy to be a part of some intrigue.

At dinner I showed Alani the letters and told her about the events of the day, but I was disappointed by her reaction. She wasn't particularly impressed. She was pushing a mushroom around her plate with her fork, not eating much.

"What's on your mind?" I asked.

"Well, while you were sleuthing today, I was ... thinking."

"Oh oh."

She smiled for a moment. The Alani from two days before.

Then she said, "I've decided that I'm not crazy about this place, Fish. This boat, these people."

"Well, it has its ups and downs."

"Downs, Fish. Mostly downs." She picked up a letter from the table. "Things like this. People grasping, pushing, hating."

"That's the world, Alani. That's not just this boat."

She looked sad. "I don't belong here, Fish. And I don't think you do either."

I looked around the room. An accumulation of several years. There was a stack of postcards in the corner of the couch, sent to the Duchess from around the world by guys on vacation. Behind me there was a bulletin board with photos of the crew hauling back a net, horsing around the deck shack, scrambling around mountains in Dutch Harbor.

The boat caught a wave and my body automatically leaned into the lee. I speared a chunk of Tonni's pickled redfish.

"I don't know where I belong, Alani. Everywhere. Nowhere. This is just a bad time we're having here. People become negative, it's like a disease. There's nowhere to go to escape. You have to find something good about each day." I held out the piece of fish. "Taste this."

She took the chunk with her delicate lips, chewed slowly.

"Delicious," she said.

I leaned forward and said, "What do you miss the most up here?"

"The most? Right now I miss my girlfriends."

I watched her. I tried not to think of Tonni's leering gossip.

I said, "What about Monique?"

"What do you know about Monique?"

"Nothing. Maybe you can tell me."

"Monique, it turns out, is wonderful. She didn't quit because of the money. She quit because Tonni bullied her, put her down every step of the way. She's been a friend. I've been bringing her food. She doesn't even want to leave her cabin until she gets to Dutch Harbor."

"Is that where you were last night?" I said this in a way that I didn't mean to.

She stared at me. Into me. She said softly, "You know why men are stupid, Fish?"

"Why?"

"Because they think that affection, or even passion between women is about eating pussy." She spat the words out. With her thumb and forefinger she made a measure of about one millimeter. "It's about that much of it, if it even happens. There's a lot more going on."

"I never said--"

"Fish," she took my hand, "I know you're not like the rest of the men on this boat, so don't fall into their bullshit. Accept me for what I am. Love me for what I am and we can share the world."

I supposed she was determined to drag me into the twenty-first century, even if kicking and screaming.

I said, "Will you sleep with me tonight?"

She smiled. Leaned closer and pressed her lips against mine. Then she said, "Come to Monique's room tonight, Fish."

After dinner we helped Gunnar pull up a thirty-five ton bag of fish. It was his biggest catch of the trip, but it didn't seem to make his life much happier. In fact he was sluggish at the controls, as if he had given up the fight altogether. Once the bag was on deck he wandered aimlessly from the window without mentioning whether we should shoot the net again after we had emptied the bag. Then Martin appeared at the controls.

Vidar handled the work pretty well, considering. I watched him carefully, and noticed just a slight hesitation here and there through the haul-back. He mainly stood, impassive against the vicious wind, a cigarette clamped in his mouth while he motioned ever so slightly to the men in the bridge behind the glass, while we ran around like mad, working the gear. I doubted anyone from the wheelhouse could tell he had been drinking. Steve especially helped to make up the difference by jumping into the action to pick up the slack, exuberant to be out of the factory for an hour or so.

During the haulback I told Taj all about the faxes from the control room. He didn't seem surprised.

"Hastings ... power-trippin fool. I just hope the office ignores the asshole," he said. Then he laughed, recalling the alarm. "Boy, was he pissed off, Fish. Started screaming soon as he hit the trawl deck. I just acted stupid, like he expects us to be. I think he bought it."

After we had shot the net Steve wanted to learn a few more knots. I discouraged him because he hadn't learned the last three I had given him.

I said, "Geez, Steve, you only *need* to know three knots out here -- the clove hitch, the sheet bend and the bowline. Everything else is just for show."

"Just show me the clove hitch again."

I showed him, but the guy was slow. It would be awhile before he picked up the finer points of his job. I could tell he didn't want to go back down to the factory, so I decided to let him help us with Tonni's groceries on the bow.

I figured Vidar would be going straight back to the sugar room and I was right, so it turned out we needed Steve anyway. Up on the bow, I let Taj drive the crane, while Steve hooked up each successive hatch. I gave Taj hand signals and after the last hatch swung open I could see straight down through four open decks to the freezer.

Tonni was already down there, dressed in an enormous freezer suit, steam blowing out through his woolen facemask. He stood on top of the first pallet with a pallet strap in his hands. I was amazed that he was doing this himself. Steve appeared seconds later in a suit he must have borrowed from the freezer crew.

He called up, "Tonni wants me down here to help."

I waved. No problem. I was half-worried the steward would have a heart attack.

The work went pretty well. I could only see one guy at a time, and they appeared to switch positions, Tonni stacking boxes of frozen meats and milk, then Steve appearing after an hour or so.

The whole job took four hours, and it was two o' clock in the morning before we were finished. All I could think about was what was going to happen after I knocked on Monique's door. I could hardly wait to get off the shift, but I thought I'd wake up Vidar in the sugar room so he could go upstairs to bed. But he wasn't there. Probably already left, I thought, and went upstairs.

I showered quickly and found myself in front of Monique's door, unable to lift a hand, nervous as hell. Down the hall I saw

Hastings' door open slowly. Shit, I thought, just what I need. But it was Vidar, emerging from the darkened chief's room with something in a small paper bag. He used the wall to steady himself twice as he moved away from me toward the other side of the ship, where he shared a cabin with his counterpart from the other shift. He hadn't seen me. It was now or not at all, I thought. I knocked, and a soft voice answered. Monique's.

The door opened from the complete darkness inside the room. My eyes weren't adjusted so I have no idea whose hand it was that led me into the cabin, but I guess it doesn't really matter. Once inside, I felt a light kiss on the back of my neck, and two pairs of hands pulling me down to the soft carpeted floor and to something entirely new indeed.

6

They had no trouble finding me. When I heard the frantic pounding on Monique's door at five A.M. the first thing I thought was that there was probably some archaic maritime law against *ménage a trois* at sea. But it was Taj.

"Get up, Fish!" he yelled through the door. "C'mon brutha, I know you're in there!"

"Sure about that?" I said, as I opened the door. I had wrapped a towel around my waist.

He glanced around the room. Alani and Monique were taking a shower. We could hear the water running.

He said, "Damn, Fish, you get any more pussy on this boat, they gonna make you a statue. Put it right up on top the wheelhouse."

I stared at him. "Taj --"

"Hey, I just don't come barging in for no good reason. Man, it's Gunnar -- he's gone!"

" Gunnar? Gone? What do you mean, *Gone*?"

"Outta here. With the skiff. Musta took it last night. Martin

83

and Jon came lookin for you, but you wasn't in your cabin. I figured I knew where you might be. Been a lot of gossip lately 'bout these girls."

"Took the skiff?" I looked at him stupidly.

"Brutha, just get your clothes on and let's go."

"But --"

"Just C'mon, man!"

I dressed and followed him outside. It was about a quarter past five. There was a light, chilly wind blowing from the west, and not a trace of morning light anywhere. The deckhands on the opposite shift were there with Martin and the captain. Someone had shifted a mounted halogen light so that it shone over the side. Everyone was leaning over the railing, looking at the waterline, where the hook from the skiff davit swung back and forth a few feet above the water, empty.

The captain straightened up to look at me. The glare behind his back made him look taller. He said, "We got you out of bed, Paul, because we need to figure out when this happened." His manner was crisp, professional. There was a sense of power in voice I had not heard before.

I looked at the men leaning against the railing. "Where's Vidar?" I asked.

Bjorn peered at me through the darkness. "He's not feeling too well this morning."

I thought about the last time I had seen him, stumbling

toward his cabin just a few hours earlier.

Jon said, "The skiff is right across the trawl deck from your deck shack, Paul. How is it that no one on your shift heard or saw the davit being moved?"

I recalled the events of the night before. I said, "There was a haulback at about eight-thirty. An hour later we were moving groceries on the bow. That lasted until two A.M. It could have happened anytime while we were on the bow, we wouldn't have heard a thing. When did you find this?"

The crew turned to Bjorn. I didn't know him well, but I knew he was the most Americanized of the bosuns. He had lived in Seattle maybe eight years. He wore his hair slicked back, and waxed and twisted his mustache. He looked like a guy that might be fun to drink with.

He spoke with almost no accent. "I noticed the davit was down when we came on at two, but we had a haulback right away. There was no time to check it out. The haulback was *all* fucked up -- a cable snapped and we lost the port bottom wing of the net. Took us hours to get it straight. It wasn't until twenty minutes ago that we got up here to see."

"But you noticed the davit at two?"

"Uh huh."

"So it could have happened anytime between nine-thirty last night and two this morning," I said.

Jon shook his head. "No. The factory manager brought some

garbage bags out to the incinerator room around midnight last night. The skiff was there. Gunnar left between midnight and two. The last two hours of your shift."

I glanced down at the empty davit, which rested in the DOWN position, leaning over the side like a giant insect. A greasy cable led down from a winch mounted on top of the tilted davit. The weighted hook was now swinging into the side of the boat, striking the steel like a bell.

Bjorn motioned to a deckhand, who winched up the cable and returned the davit to its position. As the crewman returned, he stepped over a pile of plastic garbage bags next to the controls.

I said, "Are those the bags from the factory? Didn't anyone burn them?"

Bjorn said. "We tried, but the incinerator is broken again."

This was nothing new. It seemed the damned thing broke down every other day. The garbage would pile up sometimes for a week. It was hard to keep up with, but the maritime laws for dumping plastic are severe. Anyone caught throwing garbage bags over the side was immediately fired, no matter what their position. So we let it pile up.

Jon had shifted so that he was facing all of us. He said, "Look, while we're all here, let me mention that we need to keep this to ourselves. The last thing the crew needs to know is that the fishmaster has jumped ship. Morale is low enough. Got it?"

Most of us nodded. I said, " Are you going to tell the office?"

Jon looked at me. "We haven't decided what we're going to do yet." Then he climbed back to the bridge.

Martin followed him but paused next to me. He wore a dazed expression.

I said, "You sure he was alone?"

"We don't know. Probably. His clothes are missing from his room. The pictures of his family. Tonni is mustering a crew count, just in case. Then he's checking all the cabins. He's pretending it's a drug search." He shook his head slowly. "Gunnar was in a bad way, Fish, but I never thought it would come to something like this."

"How far are we from land?"

"That's the only good thing. The Pribilof Islands are right over there, about sixty miles." He pointed toward the east, where the faintest touch of light was beginning to appear.

"If he has his wits about himself, he might have gotten there in two, three hours. If that's where he was going."

"Where else is there? " I asked, looking at the flat gray sea stretching to the horizon.

"Nowhere," is all he said as he climbed back toward the bridge.

I tried to imagine the old man, broken and irrational, pushing the skiff wildly against a dark sea of failure.

A few minutes after Martin returned to the wheelhouse, I heard the winches start up. Bjorn's crew left to get ready for a haulback. Taj and I remained alone, leaning on the railing. My watch showed six o' clock. Plenty of time for a good nap before work, but I was still curious about a few things. So was Taj.

He directed my attention to the bowline painter, a long piece of nylon rope that trailed from the front of the Duchess into the water. The painter is used when the skiff is lowered into the sea. Its function is to hold the small boat steady alongside the Duchess as she steams along, until the bosun motors the skiff forward enough to disconnect the painter. Once the davit hook and the painter are disconnected, the skiff is free from the ship. Now the painter trailed aimlessly into the water. Its end lay beneath the surface but the rope itself raised and lowered with each passing wave.

I said, "Gunnar must have cut the painter."

"I see that, Fish, but where's the end? If Gunnar cut it, why isn't it floating up on the surface?"

It was a good question, then I remembered that I had weighted the painter with a shackle a month before. The weight made it easier to lower the light nylon rope to a returning skiff on a windy day. Before I had attached the shackle, the end of the painter would blow around crazily, making it difficult for the deckhand in the skiff to grab it. The weight was a self-serving idea, since the deckhand in the skiff was usually myself.

Taj nodded as I explained, but I found myself troubled about another idea.

Skiffing is normally a three-man operation. One to lower and raise the skiff from the davit, two in the skiff itself. The bosun usually drives the small boat while a deckhand connects and disconnects the various hooks and lines. On the Duchess, the skiff davit was mounted forty feet above the water. In order for Gunnar to have taken the skiff, he needed help. At least someone to lower the boat to the water, I thought. I mentioned this to Taj.

He said, "That's the first thing I thought about this morning. How could he do it himself? But he did. Check this out."

I followed my partner down a deck level and back to the davit. Taj picked up a coil of thin twine next to the controls. He carefully tied an end to the top of the lever marked LOWER. Then he tossed the line over the side. We looked over. It reached nearly to the waterline.

"When they first told me about Gunnar, I came out here right away. This is the way it was before I came and roused you. One of the guys probably coiled this line up. But it was hangin just like it is now."

I put it together in my mind. I pictured Gunnar with his bags, tossing them into the skiff. Untying the straps. Using the controls to lower the davit to the DOWN position in order to swing the skiff out alongside the boat. Then stepping into the skiff as it hung, forty feet above the sea.

He could have tied the twine to the control lever from the skiff, or maybe before he stepped into it. It didn't matter. Once he tossed it over, all he had to do was keep a steady pull on the twine to lower himself, all the way down to the water.

"I see it," I said.

"Yep," said Taj. "When he got to the bottom, he just waited until the painter pulled tight, and slacked out the davit cable all the way. Disconnected the hook, threw it over and let it swing. Then all he had to do was go to the front of the skiff and cut the painter."

"And away he went ... " I said.

We looked east. The sky and sea came together in a perfect blend of grayness, obliterating any sign of horizon. It produced an unsettling effect in me, as if the world held no boundaries.

Taj spoke quietly, almost to himself. "Dude just flipped out, Fish. Just blew out of town like this was a train station."

I heard Bjorn's crew hauling back the net behind and below us, but I didn't turn around to watch. I was lost in thought about Gunnar, trying to imagine his state of mind, and how much pressure it would take to drive an old master away from his art. I thought about all the times that I had wanted to do the very same thing -- pack up and leave, somehow. During the worst of days, when everything you touch turns to shit in your hand, and you pray to God to let you end the shift without killing someone or yourself. But no matter how bad it got I never reached the point at which I felt I could not continue. Never to the point at which, when I added everything up, the bad far outweighed the good. And so what bothered me the most was that I could not imagine Gunnar reaching that dark place, either.

Chapter 6

But then something happened that distracted me from my doubts and made me forget all about Gunnar and his misfortune. The fish returned.

7

It was a holocaust.

I stood together with Taj, chest deep in writhing fish. Fish trying desperately to swim in a waterless sea of twisting fish bodies. Fish whose spines stretched and shook in final spasms of life and whose mouths stretched open for one more suck. Fish whose eyes clouded like marbles on a frozen sidewalk.

We were laughing.

We were laughing because we had accidently stepped off the cod end onto an open tank that we couldn't see for the mountain of pollock above it. Now we were sinking slowly and we laughed as Vidar tossed us a line and laughed with us.

The Duchess was out of room. Four tanks held nearly three hundred tons of fish, and there were sixty left in a bag we could not empty for hours.

The crew was ecstatic. It was as if a dam from the heavens had burst and was raining gold upon their heads. The factory manager graciously allowed those that quit to return to share in the bounty. They all showed up except for Monique, who was driven by an inner set of values that I had come to better understand as the three of us spent the nights together. She seemed to exist in a plane a level or two higher than any of us on the boat did – she appeared, at times, almost celestial. The way she moved and carried herself reminded me of the idealized versions of Greek Goddesses I read of as a teenager. She rarely spoke, and when she did it was with impossibly perfect diction. When Alani and I lay next to her, the three of us in an exhausted afterglow, I would sometimes picture Monique in a flowing robe, her perfect body carved from marble, with an aloof, playfully cruel manner. The fact that she looked down on all of us as if we were tiny human playthings didn't seem to bother me as much as perhaps it should have. Instead, I think I was becoming addicted to her lightest touch.

In the galley, I shared in Taj's happiness. He made over a thousand dollars that day. Yet I hid an element of cynicism. We were on an uphill leg of a cycle I had witnessed more times than I could count.

Always the same sequence of events: The fish disappear. For a half a day, the processors are relieved. They welcome the rest as medicine for an inhuman exhaustion. But after a day they begin to appear at the door leading to the trawl deck, looking anxiously out at the water. The next day they are accosting me in the galley, wringing their hands. *Where are the fish? What are you guys doing?*

By the fourth day they won't speak to me, but I overhear them at dinner, bemoaning the end of the resource. They talk about the rewards of crab processing, discuss opportunities in longlining. The first few quit that night, maybe the next morning.

When the fish return, perhaps that day, or the next, the crew is jubilant. They outline their futures in glowing and specific terms. Real estate empires are planned on mess room napkins; I find myself stumbling over stacks of magazines devoted to classic automobiles.

A week later we pull up an empty bag. And so it goes. But this time there was an added factor, at least for me. There were ideas tugging at the corners of my mind. Niggling doubts, questions that rose up at night. Where was Gunnar? There had been no word from the office. No one in the fleet had spotted a small orange boat with an old man at the wheel. And no reports from the Pribolof Islands of an old Norwegian landing out of nowhere in a 16-foot orange skiff. I seemed to be the only one concerned about him. My speculation was dismissed with a shrug. It was a subtle extension of the same lack of respect shown to processors who quit in the middle of a trip. It didn't matter what the old fisherman's state of health, he was a quitter. Even Taj said once, "Man can take care a his own self, Fish."

Besides, as Vidar pointed out, the weather had turned just about perfect. He was quite sure that Gunnar was hunched over a native bar somewhere in the islands, soaking up to forget a miserable end to his career.

Two days passed, and the luck stayed with us.

I was astounded by the transformation in our captain. It seemed he was everywhere. Downstairs, squeezing the roe from fish, laughing with the processors. He was riding a wave of hope and had proven to be a master of morale. He had begun to fish. Martin trained him for a few hours after each shift, then went to bed. Jon was catching nearly as much as Martin himself, though he was shaky with the controls during haulbacks. I was surprised to see the patience Vidar extended to the young captain, even when he jerked at cables just inches from our faces.

They told the office about Gunnar that evening, when they sent in the first decent production report. The company weighed the balance, and settled for filing a report with the coast guard. They found no reason to stop fishing.

I had to agree with that. There was nothing we could do, but wait for him to turn up.

Vidar was in the deck shack drinking a noxious mixture in a can of pop. I noticed he had become bold about it, but there was nothing for *me* to say about it. And it was remarkable how little it affected his performance. You would only notice a difference if you had worked with him for years, as I had. But Martin had too, and I assumed that his silence was based on a certain kind of respect for seniority that had its roots overseas and that I didn't understand.

In fact, Martin was making one of his rare appearances in the deck shack that day. He had brought the production reports for the past few shifts, also an exact calculation of Taj's crew share to cheer him up if he needed it. He didn't. Martin showed us how the Duchess was slowly gaining on the leaders of the fleet. It all looked very promising.

Then he was telling us about the captain.

"I won't say he's a natural, or anything, but he's got something. He's picking it up, and he hasn't smashed a net."

Taj was always quiet around people from the wheelhouse, and decided just then to immerse himself in the small project of splicing a new knife belt. Vidar had closed his eyes, but Martin took no notice of him. Martin was there to visit me.

I said mildly, "Little jumpy at the controls."

Martin wore a serious expression. "I know. We've talked about it. He knows he's nervous. I admire him for that. But he'll get it, Fish. We just have to give him time." He was searching my face for something, maybe it was acceptance of the situation as it stood. He was now the Fishmaster, and I supposed I should have felt a little better about it than I did. Maybe he sensed that.

I said, "Of course. He's been waiting a long time for this. He deserves a good chance."

"What is it you say ... his ship has come in?"

I smiled at this but I was thinking of other things.

I said, "And the sonar? How's that been?"

A flicker of annoyance crossed his face like a shadow. He said, "I don't ... I'm not sure what happened there. Have you been up to see the screen?"

I told him I had not.

"Well, it's almost solid red. You could throw a bucket over the side and catch something. So it's impossible to tell, but I sent a fax anyway, and the company is sending a technician to Dutch whenever we come in. But I can't worry about the sonar now. We're catching fish. That's all that matters."

And so it was, as always. Very little else mattered at all, when it came down to it.

Vidar had begun to snore. Martin seemed not to notice. Taj shot me a look and grinned.

"Seems strange, is all," I said.

"What?"

"I mean Gunnar. You know ... he takes off, the fish show up. If he had only waited another day--"

"You're getting obsessed with this, Fish," Martin said. "Gunnar is sick. Maybe sick in ways we don't know. I've seen stranger things happen at sea."

"Like what?"

He looked grim. "Things I don't want to have to think about. You've been with us what ... five years, now?"

"I've been with the company just as long as you have, Martin."

"I mean fishing. You've been fishing five years."

"Little more, if you count when I was just outta school, but yeah, five years."

He smiled tightly. "Give it a few more, and you'll learn to take things as they come, let them go when they go. You know what I mean?"

I nodded. Martin was a friend. But I saw that there was an element between us that I had been unable to see before, because I was so deeply involved with my own growth as a professional fisherman. Over the years he had helped me uncover a set of values I didn't know I had. This life he had delivered to me, this life at sea, contained a kind of rugged independence from which a message rang behind every ounce of fraternal love, every enjoyable moment, every blood rush of adrenaline -- the message was ... live for *now*, let the rest go. It was a sort of permanent extension of that surge of sudden freedom that came with casting off the lines and pulling slowly away from the dock, away from the myriad confusion and troubles that fester on land, in the cities and towns from which we make our own personal messes.

And so gradually I had given up a wife, a daughter, a sense of permanence. At that moment I understood that I gave up these things almost solely for the feeling of lightness that came with casting the lines from the ship and drifting slowly away toward the endless expanse that was the sea.

Now, whether he knew it or not, Martin led me further toward a way of looking at the world that was severed from any reference I had known.

I said, "I'm not sure I want to get to that point."

"What point?"

"I mean I hope I always care more about people like Gunnar than I care whether there's fish going into the net."

He stood up slowly. When he got to the door he put a foot up on the steel hatch plate and looked out at the deck. It was as if he were talking to himself.

He spoke softly. "You misunderstand me, Fish. I care about Gunnar in ways you can't possibly know. What I mean is that if you want to make it in this way of life – this career -- you can't let yourself get distracted by things that don't matter to you. You have to focus." Then he turned and said, "If you can't do that, Fish, then maybe it's best to find something else to do."

Taj spoke quietly as he finished his belt, so as not to wake up Vidar, who had slipped into the fetal position and slept soundly between us.

"Why you pushin against that man, Fish? Don't you think he got enough to think about?"

I didn't have an answer right away so I watched him at work. He spliced an eye in a piece of 3/8" nylon twine just over a meter long. When he finished he took a strip of old fire hose and rolled it into a tube wide enough to accommodate his knife. Then he wrapped the makeshift sheath tightly with electricians tape. He used the tape again to attach the sheath to the twine, then he tied the belt around around his waist. He slipped his knife into the sheath and leaned back.

"What do *you* think about Gunnar, then?"

"I don't think bout the man."

I just looked at him and he said, "And when I do, I think about a crazy old man who stole a skiff. Maybe drowned out there, or froze to death. Who knows?"

"Don't you think it's strange that the fish came back right after Gunnar disappeared? I mean, doesn't that strike you as a hell of a coincidence?"

"Man, now you startin' to look for things that ain't there. What has the fish got to do with Gunnar? Fish come and go. Wasn't it you a few days ago told me to just accept it?"

I saw his point. I was starting to feel a little foolish. Maybe I was getting paranoid. Maybe Martin was right, that I needed to focus on my job, instead of sitting around the deck shack worrying about things I had no answers for. Especially now that Vidar was, for all intents and purposes, out of commission.

We stepped out onto the deck. The cod end remained half full, the ass end unzipped and spilling fish slowly into a tank nearly filled with fish.

I said, "You been down to check the tanks?"

He looked at his watch. "Two more hours."

The Duchess had a deck wide enough to accommodate two nets at a time. Right now the starboard net was fishing, while the bag from the port side waited to be emptied. In two hours we would finish emptying the bag, zip up the end and drag it forward on the port side. Then we could haul back the starboard net, pull up a bag stuffed with a hundred tons of fish, and fasten the bag in place with chains so it didn't roll over and kill someone. Then we could shoot the empty net on the port side right away. The stuffed bag on the starboard side would then sit on deck for as long as five hours. When the fishing was that good, the fishermen were always a hundred tons ahead of the factory. After two hours of towing, Martin or Jon could haul in enough cable to raise the net above the level of the fish and pull another full bag behind us until we had room for it on the deck. It was the most relaxed kind of fishing. Everyone stayed in a good mood. No real pressure on the deck, and the processors all made money, so no whining in the galley.

But I was restless. Taj followed me as we started an informal inspection of the boat. We made it as far as the empty skiff davit, where a mountain of garbage had accumulated.

"This is ridiculous," I said.

"Smells pretty bad too."

"I can't believe no one has fixed the incinerator."

"Oh, there was quite an argument bout that yesterday."

"Oh yeah?"

"Yep. You guys were dumpin' the bag. I was back here by the net reel tryin to untie that first strap, remember?"

I nodded.

"Well, they didn't see me, but Tonni and the cap'n were up here. I guess Tonni's been wantin' this stuff burnt for a long time, now. But you know, Hastings has to fix the incinerator, and I guess he just laughs at Tonni. Don't take him seriously at all. Just says, 'I'll get to it when I get to it.' You know how he is."

"My buddy."

Chapter 8

"Well, Tonni is up here complainin' about Hastings, actually comin' down kinda hard on the cap'n, tellin him to get his ass down there, get Hastings in gear --"

"He said that? He said, 'Get your ass --'"

"Well, it started like that, with Tonni in control and everything, then the cap'n comes up tough and says somethin like 'It's not my station to deal with the garbage situation on this ship. That's your responsibility.' I thought Tonni was going drop dead right there, then the cap'n says, "And it's not your station to tell me how to do my job.' Holy shit, Fish, Tonni just blew up. I mean he turned three colors to purple. Looked like a Sumo wrestler. I thought he was gonna kill the man. He screamed, 'You think you're the goddamned captain or something!?'"

"He said that?"

"Sure did. And you know what, Fish. I couldn't believe it, but Jon just looked at him like he was a bug. Cold, like the ice on the bow right now." Taj looked at me. "That man has changed, Fish."

"Uh huh ... so what else?"

"Well, I had to go down and help you hook up the last strap, so I didn't hear nothin' else, but when I came back it looked like Tonni was 'bout ready to cry. Then the cap'n put his hands on Tonni's shoulders and said somethin' quiet, then he left. Tonni looked a little better but I'd say there were about fourteen emotions comin' through that face when he left. Now you see this pile here, so I guess not much was accomplished by the whole exercise."

"Why didn't you tell me this before, Taj?"

"What for? You know I don't spread boat gossip 'round. I just hang back, soak it all in. *Ou te se tagata tau suati*," he said and smiled.

"Yeah ... you've said that before. Well, you hear anything like that again, let me know, will you? I get curious about these kind of things."

"You curious bout a lot of things, Fish. It's gonna get you in trouble. Ain't no business of ours what goes on up there in that bridge."

I shook my head. "Don't you think it's better we know what's going on around here? What about the faxes from Hastings? Aren't you glad we know about that?"

Taj rubbed his chin, glancing at me from the corner of his eye. For some reason I wanted his approval on this. I felt like I needed someone on my side.

He said, "When I was growin' up on the island we had a little group of friends we liked to call a gang. We never hurt nobody, just hung out, hustling basketball, some rugby sometimes. Anyway, one day we saw a man get killed. Just outside a bar. Man came right out and shot him dead in the street. When the cops came round askin' questions none of us said a word. I went home that night and told my *Ta'ma* and he said I done the right thing. Said if it aunt your business, don't make it so. You run into trouble every time."

Chapter 8

Taj must have seen the disappointment in my face. He said, "Now I've always lived by that, but you my deck partner, Fish. I don't know you all that well, but if I can help you out without us getting' in trouble, I guess I don't see no problem in that."

I smiled at him. "Sounds good to me, Taj. Thanks."

"No problem. Now what we gonna do 'bout this garbage?"

Sometimes when you walk into a room you get a certain kind of feeling. Like maybe the occupants have just finished having oral sex, or smoking crack or something. A sense of guilt hangs in the air, and for a split second there is a mixture of embarrassment and curiosity, as if you just missed something you shouldn't have seen, but that might have been interesting.

That's how I felt when I stepped into the control room to see Hastings about the garbage. But I couldn't imagine anyone giving Hastings a blow job, and if there was one thing he wasn't, it was a crack head.

He had been at the computer the moment before I came down the stairs and opened the door. The screen was blank but it still glowed a little as he shuffled to the other side of the narrow room. He moved in such a way that I knew it was a distraction. But what confused me for a moment was that he wasn't alone. There was a young guy with a stupid expression on his face standing by the door at the far end of the control room. He was holding a cardboard tube of red grease and had rags sticking out of the pockets of his coveralls. Then I remembered who he was.

The day after I pilfered Hastings' garbage can he had pulled two brainless kids from the factory, given them grease guns, and designated them "oilers." He put them on a twelve-on/twelve-off schedule to cover both his shift and that of the first engineer. Everyone had laughed at the appointments, which were seen as a way for him to spend more time doing nothing, but I suspected that Hastings had missed the garbage and wanted someone in the control room every minute of the day. And sure enough, over the past few days, every time I needed a tool from the engine department, there was either Hastings at his desk, or a kid sitting around the control room with a backwards baseball cap reading a BIG TRUCK magazine.

Just now I had the feeling that the oiler had stepped into the room about the same time as I, pinning Hastings between us.

The kid said in a dull voice, "I finished the rotor, Mr. H, now should I do the factory bearings?"

"Mr. H?" I said. I looked at Hastings. I was almost laughing.

The engineer pulled back a tight grin. He stared at me through his coke bottles as he answered the kid. "Yes, Bob. The factory bearings."

When the kid left Hastings said, "Don't try to embarrass me in front of people like that."

"Sorry, Hastings, couldn't help it."

"What do you want, Saxon?" Sounded like he drank too much coffee that morning.

I moved so that I could see the computer at the same time as I faced him. I said, "You got a serious problem with the garbage, Hastings."

He smirked. "That's your problem, not mine. I'll get to the incinerator when I have time."

"Been busy, lately?"

He was gritting his teeth. "You don't know what busy is, Saxon. You guys sit up there and nap all day. How many haulbacks have you had this shift?"

I ignored the question. I looked for a disc sticking out of the computer drive, but there was none. The drive port was open, too.

I said, "Vidar sleeps, not me."

He snorted, "Vidar drinks, and sleeps."

My gaze fell for an instant to the front pocket of his coveralls, where he kept a pack of cigarettes. There was a square impression pressing against the pocket on the outside of the pack. About the size and shape of a computer disc.

I said, "Yeah, funny about that."

"What?"

"Well, Vidar never drank on the boat before. It's a dry boat anyway. I can't imagine where he's getting the stuff, can you?"

"I don't have time to worry about the personal problems of drunken Norwegians. And I don't have the time to sit here and chat, so if you will excuse yourself, I will get back to work."

I headed slowly for the door. Before I left, I stopped and said, "Don't sweat the garbage problem, Hastings, I was only doing you a favor by coming down here."

"How's that?"

"A little while ago the boat listed pretty heavily to the port side. A few plastic bags fell overboard. The captain happened to be looking out just then. I think his exact words were, "Get that fucking engineer up here to fix that incinerator. Now."

"Oh."

I nodded soberly. It was a lie, but I doubted Hastings could check it without making himself look like more of a fool than he was.

I said, "Captain's been pretty serious lately. I'd maybe put that job on your agenda. Hell, I'll even give you a hand."

I wasn't surprised when Hastings showed up minutes later. From the shack I watched him place his tools next to the incinerator. Then he stepped into the entrance leading to the cabins beneath the wheelhouse. Taj just stared at me as I flew from the room.

I made it to the doorway as he turned the corner at the end of the hall. I followed, and peered around the bulkhead as he unlocked the door to his cabin. As he pushed into the room I saw that the computer disc was still in his pocket.

He left the door open slightly. I saw the light go on, and heard him moving inside the cabin. When the light clicked off and his hand appeared on the outside edge of the doorframe I hurried back to the deck. By the time he returned to the incinerator room I was sitting again in the deck shack.

Taj said, "Man, you bored, or somethin?"

I smiled. "Nah. In fact I gotta go help the chief right now."

I wasn't much help, really. I just handed him the occasional tool, held a few wires in place while he tested them with a voltmeter. It's surprising how two people who don't get along can forget their differences when there's something to do together. But I wasn't there for altruistic purposes. Long before we were finished I confirmed that the pocket in his coveralls held nothing more than a   pack of cigarettes.

10

The scene remains in my memory like a small thing of beauty you keep locked in a glass cabinet. Something you take out once in a while to dust off and look at simply for the pleasure it gives you:

I am lying on my back on a pile of soft cushions. Monique is somewhere below my field of vision, treating my erection like a kitten she's rescued from a bulldog. Alani is sitting lightly, very lightly, on my upper lip. She tastes salty and sweet. She is leaning forward and down toward Monique. She is trembling. I can't see what she is doing, but I can imagine.

Toward the end of early morning, when it was time for Alani and me to sleep for a few hours before returning to work, the three of us lay among the cushions spread around the floor, and talked. Alani used her lover's smooth belly as a pillow and stared up at the ceiling. I was holding Monique's impossibly delicate foot in my lap.

"Were you raised in 19th century Japan, or what?"

Monique's laughter sounded like rain hitting glass. She said nothing.

Alani said dreamily, "Monique was raised on a tiny tropical island on the other side of the world. Her mother put orchids in her hair every morning of her life and she swam in water as clear as diamonds."

She twisted her head back. "Right?"

Monique said, shortly, "I was born in Brooklyn."

When we stopped laughing we lay for a minute and listened to the distant grinding sound of the winches starting to move. The noise brought me back to the reality of the boat.

Alani said, "Have you noticed how the people stare now?"

"We're an exotic species," I said.

"The first few days were the worst," said Alani. "I could walk into the mess room and I swear you would hear a pin drop for a full minute. Than a little bit of low talk and an explosion of laughter from a table. Lots of grinning faces I couldn't bear to look at, they were so ugly. It was torture."

Monique, who hadn't left the room since she quit, said, "Imagine living in a little town in North Dakota. There's only a hundred people, so the whole village is smaller than a city block. It's so small, in fact, that everybody works in one big room, eats in another big room, but for privacy they go into little rooms to sleep. You can't leave the town because there's been a disaster and there's no more world out there, so you stay on and on, and feed off each other, like vampires. And one day there's no more blood left. Then you all die."

Alani shuddered. "God, Monique."

I barely heard the exotic woman whisper above the sound of the hydraulics. She stroked her lover's hair, and said, "You should tell him, Alani."

Alani looked up at me with fathomless black eyes. She was biting her lower lip, and her small front teeth practically glowed against the olive color of her skin.

"Fish ... I'm ... Monique and I are leaving when we get to the dock."

It was hard for me to tell what was quieter -- the silence in the room or the vacuum that seemed to form in my head at hearing this piece of news, although it didn't take me completely by surprise. There is an end to everything, it seems. Even this. Especially this.

"I know," I said. "I've known it, I think."

Monique looked over Alani's profile at me. Our eyes were on the same level. She said, "We want you to come with us."

I stared at a point a mile behind her. We were in the middle of a season that would last until March. I had signed an annual contract two weeks before, accepting with gratitude a raise to over three hundred a day from a company to which I had been loyal for five years. There were a hundred factory trawlers, dozens of companies, but not a lot of jobs like mine. And there was the sea. This ocean beneath us, a roadless infinity to anywhere, nowhere, and away. For me it was the essence of an existential freedom that I had already chosen over love once before. Was anything different this time?

"Where would we go?" I asked, but it wasn't really a question.

Alani sat up. "Fish, we'd go to that island! Where Monique was raised."

I smiled sadly. In her simple way Alani had defined the relationship. A bright dream in a small room, created out of hope and darkness. Like a painting by a prisoner on death row.

"We'll see what happens," I said, but by the way they looked at me there was no reason for me to say anything. I reached for Alani's ankle and gave a little squeeze.

Monique yawned and settled back against a cushion. She closed her eyes. We were all getting bleary. Before we went to sleep I needed something from Alani.

I whispered in her ear, "Can you get me a master key, beautiful?" Even after the three of us had begun to sleep together, Alani and I continued to use terms of endearment that we didn't share with Monique. Neither seemed to mind.

Alani's small mouth pulled down at the corners. "Tonni's got it around his neck, Fish."

"All the time?"

"I bet he sleeps with it."

"Who else has one?"

She shrugged. Yawned and stretched. Her eyes were getting heavy. "Oh ... the captain, probably the chief."

Forget those two, I thought. Monique's breathing grew steady and soft, and I absently rested a hand on her thigh.

"What happens when you need to open a door -- like the laundry room?"

She didn't answer, so I nudged her.

"Fi-ish... stop."

"Sweetheart, I need your help. This is important." I kissed her behind her ear and she opened her eyes. Giggled.

"What's so important?"

"I need to get into the chief's room."

"Why?"

"I don't know yet. And it's probably best you don't know anything about it."

"Fish, what's going on?" Alani was whispering now.

"I think the chief ... look, isn't there a time when you need to unlock a door? Don't you ever have to get the key from Tonni?"

"Baby, I don't care about what goes on this goddamned boat, anyway, so I don't care if you don't want to tell me, but just promise me you won't do anything stupid, okay?"

"Alani, that's one thing I can never promise anyone."

She sighed. "When I need to unlock a door, Tonni comes and unlocks it. Then he locks it again after I'm done."

"Trusting guy, huh? What if he's busy?"

"If he's busy, I don't ask him."

I was quiet for a moment, trying to figure out a way, when she said, "Once, when he was in a terrible mood, I asked, and he threw the key at me. Screamed to get my ass back in two seconds flat or I'd be sitting in here with Monique until February."

"Nice guy, too."

"Fish, I think he's manic depressive. One minute he's laughing, witty -- really sweet and funny -- next he's coming down your throat."

"What was he so angry about?"

"Oh, he had created an incredible pastry dish to bring up to the captain and he left the galley for a little while. He must have forgot or something because when he got back it was this black, smoking thing that looked like it came from the wrong end of a sick horse. He just completely lost it."

"And threw the key away like a piece of candy."

She shook her head. "More like a baseball."

"Uh huh... Do me a favor, sweetheart?"

"Anything."

"Burn something tomorrow?"

11

Our plan was for Alani to get the key from Tonni any way she could. She decided to wait until he was at his busiest, just before dinner. We hoped that managing both the cooking and the assistant's job would make it impossible for him to leave the galley, even to unlock a door for Alani. Then she could run up to the chief's room, unlock the door, and return immediately. I would slip in when I could.

The problem was that it turned out to be a busy shift. Bjorn had left us a list of small jobs his crew hadn't finished. It was about four P.M. and Taj and I were by the skiff davit, throwing the last few bags into the incinerator. Vidar was sitting in the deck shack, staring at the wall.

We had three bags left when we heard the whoosh of the flame dying, then the buzzer sounded, indicating that the burner was shut down. Another job for the engineer. Taj was holding his nose against the smell and he cursed through his woolen mitten.

"Goddamn, Fish, we almost made it."

The reek had become unbearable as we reached the last and oldest bags at the bottom of the pile. I said, "What's in those last three? If it's organic, it's going over, plastic bag or not."

Taj tore open the first two. "Last year's dinner. Damn, this shit is from another planet. *Se unavau!* "

I grabbed the bags and ripped them in half over the side. Thirty pounds of black moldy goo dropped into the water like rocks. I tossed the empty bags into the incinerator. I smiled at Taj through the stench.

He said, "Birds probably dyin behind us."

He opened the last bag. "Clothes. Just old clothes. We can leave these 'til your buddy comes up again." He threw the bag into the corner. Then he said, "Who's been splicin?"

"Huh?"

He picked up a pair of gloves that had been lying under the last bag.

"Let me see."

They were a pair of rubber deck gloves covered with black grease. I turned them in my hands. The grease was only on the palm side.

It was what happened to gloves when a deckhand spliced an eye in new cable. The stains were unavoidable, and often in the winter, when the cable grease was thickest, you just threw away the gloves.

I shrugged. "Must be the other shift. But I didn't see any new work lying around. Strange."

"Ah, you know that man Bjorn he always runnin round like a maniac, thinkin up jobs for fun. Probly had em splicing new sweeps for the nineteen ninety-five season."

I laughed and dropped the gloves onto the bag in the corner. It was a little odd but nothing I had time to worry about.

I said, "I gotta disappear in a little while for a few minutes. Can you cover for me, case Vidar comes out of his trance, decides to do something?"

He frowned. "What you doin now?"

I explained my suspicions, which were vague, to say the least.

Taj stared at me. "So you gonna break into the chief's room, and search for somethin you don't even know what it is? And for what reason? Just because you had a feelin when you was down in the control room yesterday? You maybe feelin a little bit ill?"

I grinned. "Look, it's probably nothing. Maybe I'm crazy, but I have to check this out. I'll be out in a minute."

"When you goin in?"

"I don't know. Soon, I hope.

Taj rolled his eyes. "Well, you know I'll back you up. But I got no sympathy you lose your job. Fact, I guess it'll be my job then, won't it?"

We were on the upper stern deck, moving around some bales of net web, when Alani appeared in the doorway beneath the wheelhouse.

I waved and she was gone.

"That's it, Taj. Later."

He shook his head. "Keep on thinkin, boss. *Upu faifai ...*"

I shrugged at him. He waved me away. I guessed that was one saying I would have to look up when I got home.

The light was on when I pushed open Hastings' door. I was surprised by what I found. Considering the condition of the control room, I had expected a dump. The chief engineer had one of the most spacious cabins on the boat, and he kept it like a banker's office.

A laptop computer rested on a wide desk along the forward bulkhead. Just above it there was a set of glass-faced shelving that held rows of technical manuals and a few video tapes I recognized from the downstairs lounge. On the far corner of the desk a TV/VCR was pointed at the couch on the other side of the cabin. There was a science magazine on the table in the middle of the room and also a bowl of fruit. No bananas.

There was a bathroom about the size of my cabin and a bedroom with a bed that pulled out double. I decided to save those rooms for last.

It searched the room for fifteen frantic minutes before I found the computer disc. It was wedged between two manuals in the bookcase that I had gone over three times in my haste. I needed to take a course in this kind of thing.

When I saw the initials RC-S marked on the disc, I knew what it was even before I slipped it into the laptop. The screen came on and a window jumped up automatically. I used the mouse to pull the program up. It was a file of commands written in some obscure programming language, so I could barely understand it, but there were enough clues for it to be pretty obvious -- a recalibration program for the sonar unit.

I shut off the computer and slipped the disc into my pocket. As I moved toward the door I became aware of a smell that had been just on the edge of my attention the whole time I had been in the room. It was a familiar smell and in a minute or so I knew what it was.

Hastings' room was on the forward corner of the house, and had two large portholes covered with thick curtains. I drew aside one of the curtains to find that Hastings had removed the porthole hatch altogether. In its place was a ten gallon plastic jug wedged into the sill, with a thin rubber hose leading out and a tube attached to a sealed glass bottle half-filled with clear liquid. A still. I closed the curtain and pushed the bottle back behind the cloth.

I was patting myself on the back for my cleverness when the door opened.

Hastings stepped into the room in his awkward way and when he saw me he stopped like he had hit a wall. He stared for a moment and I watched his face change from shock to fear to rage in about two seconds. His mouth was quivering and a drop of spit landed next to his shoe. His words came in a crazy rush.

"Y-You! I knew it. You sonofabitch, Saxon, you are finished.

You stole some papers from my office downstairs! Don't think I didn't miss them. Now here you are, snooping around in an officer's room. Boy, have you blown it. You are fucking history, friend." He stared at me through those glasses with triumph.

There wasn't a thought in my head. I tossed him across his room like a sack of potatoes.

Strength is a funny thing. Ask anyone who works with their hands. I'm not a big guy at all. Maybe five-eight after a good stretch. If I'm one-sixty I'm fat. But you go to work every day, move heavy things around with your body all the time without thinking about it, you'll be surprised at what you become. Then when it comes time to move something like Hastings around, it won't take much effort at all.

He hit the edge of the desk and bounced into the far wall. I followed him over, slowly. He started to say something like "You're cra--" when I picked him up and threw him across the room again.

I guess I was upset. He was silent when I approached the second time. Just stared up at me, white as old ice. There was a trickle of blood from the corner of his mouth. Must have bit his tongue or something.

I squatted down. "No, Hastings, you're finished. You drove Gunnar off this ship, ruined an old man's life, maybe killed him. Maybe he's frozen out there, drifting around dead in a little boat like an unburied Viking. And now you're poisoning the best deck boss in the Bering Sea. You're killing him, too. You're a murderer,

Hastings."

"You're nuts, Saxon. What the hell are you talking about?"

I stepped over to the window, threw aside the curtain. He looked at the still like it was something he didn't want to see.

He nodded slowly, dabbed at the blood on his chin and wiped his hand on his coveralls. He groaned a little as he got up and slid onto the couch.

He said quietly, "You're a fool. I used to think that you had some intelligence. But you can't even see what's in front of your own face. That stuff is helping you more than anyone else on this ship."

"I know what you're saying Hastings. But I don't need a promotion right now, thank you. I'll make deck boss when it's time. I'll wait for it like everyone else."

"You'll wait forever, idiot. Don't you see that? These Norwegians are taking jobs. This country's in the middle of a recession and we've got foreign nationals that make enough in a single month to support a family in Utah for a year."

"And your answer is to drive them off any way you can, is that it?"

He gestured toward the still. "It's crude, yes, but it'll do the trick. I haven't seen Vidar on deck except for haulbacks for three days. It's only a matter of time."

I wanted to hit him, but I took a breath instead. I said, "And what about Gunnar?"

He sneered, "What about him? An old man who flipped out and stole the skiff. Couldn't handle the pressure from the office. His time was up. It proves my point, doesn't it?"

I pulled the disc from my pocket and tossed it onto the table. Hastings collapsed a little when he saw it. He reached out a hand but I had him by the wrist before he was a foot from the edge of the table. I bent the wrist backward until he screamed. Then I slipped the disc back into my pocket.

I was still holding him. Bearing down with some weight. "When did you do it, Hastings? Offload? One night when no one was in the bridge? Or did you do it right in front of their noses? They'd never know, would they?" I pushed him back into the couch. He rubbed wrist and glared at me like a spoiled kid.

"I didn't have to go to the bridge," he said sullenly. "The computer in the control room is networked with the one in the wheelhouse. It was just a matter of reprogramming the sonar, but I had to create a program based on the existing file. Reverse Engineered it." I detected a hint of pride, bravado. "It took awhile, but it worked."

"So you made it so they couldn't see the fish. So the boat would catch nothing while everybody else caught a fortune. That way Gunnar would lose his job. I read that fax. You have friends you'd like to bring up here. You wanted complete control of the ship."

"No, Saxon. You have it wrong. Those friends of mine

deserve good jobs in a country they grew up in, catching fish fifty miles from their own coast. I don't care who's running this ship, so long as they're not from some two-bit country. Nothing has changed with the Norwegians in a thousand years. They still sail around the world like Vikings and rape and pillage, only now they do it with tricky lawyers and dummy corporations. When they're done here, they'll go to South America. Then New Zealand."

"What were you doing with this disc when I walked in yesterday?"

"When?"

"Don't play stupid. There's no point. I mean when I came in to ask about the garbage."

"Oh. I was just putting the finishing touches on the recalibration, getting it back to the original."

"So you waited for Gunnar to disappear, then you set it back up so Jon could catch fish, huh? Make him look good."

"Yes. But it wasn't complete. Fortunately there was so much fish he couldn't miss. But I needed to change a few more things. Look how well he's fishing now."

"Oh, he's a champ. A star. You know, Hastings, you're a sick man. You don't feel the slightest remorse over the fact that you've destroyed a man's life. That he's maybe dead or dying out there so your golden boy can have his day in the sun. And why didn't you pick on Martin -- oh yeah, that's right, he's an American citizen, even if he did spend his life in Norway. So he's okay. You're a goddamned xenophobe, Hastings. It's you that belongs in a cage, not the deckhands."

"I never expected Gunnar to do what he did. I ... I feel bad for the old man. I do. It didn't work exactly as I had planned." He looked at the floor. His face had softened a bit. It actually looked genuine and for a millisecond I almost felt sorry for him. Almost.

"Well, considering that you've cost the company a couple million bucks, I guess you're in a little trouble. Maybe they'll let you make payments."

He looked up. "What are you going to do?"

"First, this." I leaned toward the plastic still in the window and hammered at it with my fist. It dented deeply, slid a little and finally tumbled into the sea. Icy air rushed into the room. Vidar was officially cut off from the juice that was likely killing him.

"Fix your window, Hastings." I walked across the room. He watched from the couch, looking dejected and a bit nervous.

At the door I said, "I'm not sure what I'll do about this disc, Hastings. Nothing, right now. But you understand one thing before I'm outta here."

"What?"

"You're working for me now."

12

That night I mentioned nothing to the women. When she asked, I told Alani I was mistaken, and I knew Monique didn't care one way or another. Neither did Alani, except that she was concerned, I suppose, about my welfare. These two were leaving in a couple of weeks, and they were in love. The three of us had cut ourselves off from the social structure of the boat and I was reluctant to disrupt our idyll with a sad and irrelevant story.

Besides, I didn't want them involved, because I was starting to have a bad feeling. Like maybe there was more to the whole thing than Hastings' misguided nationalism. I needed to think about it, but what I did instead was fool around a lot and drift off to a nice deep sleep. Which was fine.

Taj and I talked about my encounter with Hastings as we replaced some chafing gear on the port side cod end. I kneeled on the soft web of the cod end itself and tied the plastic hairlike rope to the outside layer. It protects the bag against wear from the stern ramp and steel deck as the cod end is hauled onto the boat. It also helps in the unlikely event that the bag touches the ocean bottom. The people who manufacture the stuff have a sense of humor, I guess, because it comes in every color of the rainbow and it makes a full cod end look like a huge exotic caterpillar inching its way onto the deck.

The weather had turned cold again, but the sea remained fairly calm despite a steady breeze. The image of Taj with the hatchet, chopping the chafing rope into five-foot sections against a thick piece of teflon resting on a wooden block, steam rising from his heated breath in a great cloud, reminded me of my father chopping kindling on a New England winter morning.

Through the cold and through a light snow that was falling I heard Alani's voice calling from a distance. Turned out she was just a few steps below the wheelhouse, near the mounted life rafts, but she seemed so far because a wind from the starboard side was blowing her words away.

When she reached the deck she said, "They found it!"

I looked up at her and said, "Found what?" Taj stopped chopping.

"The skiff. I was vacuuming the radio room when the satellite phone rang, so I stopped and found Jon to answer it. He didn't tell me to leave so I sat there and listened for awhile. Then when he was finished I decided to clean the inside of the windows while they talked about it."

"My little sleuth." I felt my skin stretch tight as I grinned against the cold.

She smiled. "I knew you'd be interested."

Taj laughed shortly. "Fish, he interested in everything. *Upu fai--*"

I cut him off. "Yeah, yeah ... *Upu whatever the fuck ...*" I looked up at her, expectantly.

She said, "The call came in from a tribal cop on the island of St. Paul. I guess the skiff just washed up against their breakfront."

"Empty?"

She nodded. I had been to that tiny island a few years before. Vidar and I had to run an injured deckhand in to catch the cargo flight down to Dutch Harbor. The island was long, low and flat, with a hill on one end where the town itself was clustered. There were no trees, except a few stunted pines someone had brought from the mainland, but which barely hung on through the brutal winters. The people were mostly Aleuts, and I remembered an old Russian Orthodox church, white paint peeling, standing at the highest point in town. The islanders had built an impressive breakfront out of big black volcanic boulders. The breakfront protected the harbor and made it possible the Bering Sea crab fleet to do business there during the season. I tried to imagine the orange skiff, twisted and smashed against the dark rocks.

"No sign of Gunnar?"

"None. Just the skiff. Jon and Martin think he might have capsized or swamped on the way in. The coast guard has started a search for the body."

I sighed. "It's possible. There's some heavy rollers as you approach the mouth of the harbor. There was a wind that night, too. Seems strange that they didn't find it until today, though."

Alani hugged her herself against the cold. She said, "I guess they've had some bad weather. Also, I heard Jon say to Martin that they found the skiff in a place no one ever goes. Way off to the side, away from the mouth of the harbor."

Taj said, "Now that seem strange to me."

I shrugged. "I don't know. It might not mean anything. Tide could have pulled it."

"That's just what Martin said."

Taj said, "But why would Gunnar try for the harbor durin' a storm? He had had plenty of gas, probably had enough clothes. Why not just go to the lee side and wait it out?"

I said, "Yeah, that's true. Course, he wasn't thinking too clearly."

"Clearly 'nough to get there, though."

"Mm." I turned to Alani. "Did they say anything about the skiff itself? Like was it smashed up pretty bad, or upside down?

"Jon asked if it was upside down. It wasn't. I think the cop told him it was salvageable."

Alani shivered then and said, "I have to go, or I'll freeze out here."

"Thanks, babe."

She bent forward. Kneeling, I came nearly to her chin.

"Kiss, please." she said.

"Always."

Taj and I took a break in the deck shack. I wanted to warm up enough so I could at least think for a few minutes.

The fishing had fallen off a little. Earlier in the shift, before we started on the chafing, Martin had called to say that there would be no haulback until eight or so. Which was a good thing because Vidar hadn't bothered to show up for work at all that afternoon. I wondered how he would take the news that the well had dried up.

But I was less concerned about Vidar than about my growing suspicion about the entire skiff incident. I felt like an accumulation of doubts were pushing me in a direction I didn't want to go, toward an understanding too dark to imagine.

When we were warm, Taj and I put away the chafing rope and tools and climbed the flight of stairs to the skiff davit. We leaned against the railing on the other side of the life rafts, about thirty feet forward of the davit itself. It was the same place we stood the night of Gunnar's disappearance.

I said, "Taj, I want to look at this another way."

He gave me an amused, sideways look. "How you wanna look at it?"

"Okay, the way we figured out how Gunnar took the skiff was

by pretending we were Gunnar trying to steal the skiff, right?"

"Yup."

"Well, let's look at it like this. We don't want to steal the skiff, we just want to release it from the ship."

"Why?"

"Doesn't matter why. Let's just see if it's possible to release the boat without going with it."

Taj peered at me. "Man, you got some strange ideas in your head sometimes. Okay, though, I'll play. First thing, we swing it out, drop it down."

"Right. But it's connected in two places. At the hook from the davit crane, and from the painter on the front of the skiff. The painter leads a hundred feet forward to the bow of the ship. And you're looking down at this from up here. Now how are you going to get down there to unhook it and then get back onto the Duchess?"

Taj stared at the wake kicked up from the ship. He said, "Well, it'd be easier to go the same way as if we were stealin' the skiff. Tie a little line to the handle here, get into the boat, pull on the line and I'm in the water."

I nodded. "Okay, now you're at the bottom. You're in the skiff, and you need to disconnect the hook and cut the painter. The Duchess is going four knots, and the painter is stretched tight, holding you alongside the ship. Let's say you cut the painter first. What happens?"

Taj frowned. "If I cut the painter first, I just blew it, 'cause the skiff floats back until the hook takes the weight. Now there ain't no way to disconnect the hook. I'm stuck."

"Right. So that's out. The only other way is to disconnect the hook first. So you slack it down and disconnect it. Now you just have to cut the painter."

"Sure. But then I float away. How'm I gonna get back on the boat?"

"Have a rope tied from up here?"

Taj looked around. "Ain't nothin to tie to, Fish, except the handle and that'd break right off."

"I know it. So there's only one way left."

"What?"

"The davit cable itself." I picked up the greasy deck gloves from where we'd found them the day before. "Remember these? I checked with Bjorn. No one's been splicing cable. They were laying right here next to the davit. Right where someone would have dropped them if after they had climbed up the cable."

Taj stared at me and then looked over the side. Then he looked at the painter, part of which still trailed beneath the wake of the boat, then he looked for a long time at the davit. Then he said,

" Maybe. But there's a couple of things."

"Like what?"

"Well, I'm in the skiff, I take the hook off. Now I'm gonna cut the painter and just as I'm floating away I just sorta jump on and hope I can climb forty foot up a greasy cable? Sound a little fantastic to me."

I shook my head. "Doesn't have to be that way. What if you disconnect the hook, then climb up the cable, leave the skiff tied to the painter."

"Then what?"

"Cut the painter from up here."

"How?"

I smiled. "This is something that has bothered me from the first day, but I couldn't see until now. In fact, it was you that pointed it out. Look at the painter. Under water."

"You already explained that. You said you put a shackle on to--"

"I know. But if you wanted to cut the painter from up here you'd have to climb closer to the bow to where you could reach it. That's way past where I tied the weight. You'd take a grapple and lift the middle of the painter until you could cut it. Then good-bye skiff."

"That's right! Now you just tie on another shackle or any kind of weight and drop it in. Nobody sees the end, so nobody knows how long it is."

"Yes. I suppose we could retrieve the painter from the bow and look at the length, but it really wouldn't prove anything. I mean, if Gunnar did take the skiff it's possible that he motored forward and cut it in the middle. Not likely, but possible."

Taj said, "Well, I said there was a couple of things. The other is -- why? Why would Gunnar bother with it? You sayin he's hidin somewhere on the boat?"

"No. Gunnar couldn't climb up that cable on his best day."

Taj nodded. *"O le upega le talifau."*

"Which means ...?" I looked at him.

Taj smiled. "Means he's old, Fish."

I nodded slowly, but stared past the deckhand. I felt a sense of dread spreading across my chest.

"We don't really have any answers about this, Taj. Right now this is just speculation."

My partner gave me a doubtful look. "You mean we been up here freezing our asses off about a theory that we can't even prove?"

"No," I said slowly, still thinking, "There's a way to prove it ... but we need some help from Hastings."

Alani was standing among piles of folded clothes in the laundry room. It was warm, and a soapy chemical smell hung heavy in the air. I asked her to run up to the bridge and see if she could get a name and number for the tribal cop from St. Matthew that delivered the news. I folded clothes while I waited. She returned in twenty minutes. Jon was fishing and Martin was in bed, so she managed to get both the telephone and fax number without notice, but on the way out she had to endure a fifteen minutes of sexual innuendo from the captain. Boring, she said.

The cop's name was Nick Nixie. I recognized the last as an Eskimo surname common in Nome. I thought it odd that he worked in the islands.

I left Taj in the shack cradling a hot cup of coffee while I headed down toward the engine department. In the control room one of the oilers sat at in a chair on the wrong side of Hastings' desk, chomping gum and playing a pocket video game. He wore headphones and a walkman was clipped to the lapel of his coveralls. Some kind of metal thrash romper stomper punk music leaked out of his head, which bobbed like one of those plastic drinking Woody Woodpeckers.

I lifted one of the phones and said, "Where's Mr. H?"

He shrugged a big shrug.

I said, "Go find him."

He opened his mouth wide to speak. The gum, bright green, stuck to a top molar. "Mr. H. don't want nobody --"

I held up a hand. Stop. He stopped. I said, "Kid, go find your boss."

He looked at me. Shrugged another big shrug and stepped into the engine room. Then he stepped back in and found a pair of mickey mouse ear protectors and left again.

A few minutes later Hastings returned with the kid in tow. He wore an expression that was unreadable, but his manner was polite.

"What is it, Saxon?"

I glanced at the oiler.

Hastings said, "Bob, go do something."

"What?"

Hastings pulled the headphones down. "Go away, Bob."

The kid smiled and blew a green bubble. He picked up his grease gun at the door and bobbed out of the room.

"I need to send a fax."

"To where? And for what purpose?"

"Never mind. In fact, you can't read it. Or the answer. You just show me how the machine works down here with the satellite phone and I'll send it myself. And I need the number for this machine."

I saw him frown behind his beard. "What are you up to, Saxon?"

"That's none of your business. At least for your sake I hope it isn't. Now move it. I'm in a hurry."

He pulled a nasty grin. "Busy, I take it."

"Yeah. I need to get back to my nap. Hastings, don't fuck with me. You know what's what."

He scowled, and leaned over the machine. It was a simple operation. I told him to get lost and he walked to the other side of the control room and glared at me. I wrote my message by hand in a sheet of white lined paper from his desk:

To: Nick Nixie,

From: Jon Elliot, Captain F/T Northern Duchess

RE: URGENT! PLEASE RESPOND IMMEDIATELY

Mr. Nixie: I am sending this fax because our satellite phone is out of commission. We have an auxiliary system for our fax machine so we may receive your reply as soon as possible via the above number.

Regarding our skiff that we spoke about earlier, I need to know two very important details about the condition of the skiff. The answers are critical to our understanding of what happened on this end. Please respond immediately if this is convenient.

#1 **How long, in feet, is the painter line, if there is one attached, on the front of the skiff?**

#2 **Please determine the fuel level of the skiff.**

Thank you very much.

I signed the captain's name and sent it off. Then I sat back in Hastings' chair and waited. We stared at each other for a few minutes, then he snarled, "Do you mind?"

I got up and gave him his chair and then parked myself in front of the machine. I looked at my watch. Five-thirty. I hoped I had caught Nick Nixie. There was no way to know what hours they kept on St. Paul. He might have hung up with Jon earlier and gone straight home to a happy wife and some walrus stew. Or he might even work out of his home. Probably in a cozy house overlooking the sea. St. Paul's remoteness was beautiful in an exotic kind of way. At that moment I envied the guy. Or my idea of what he was, what I imagined he had.

Hastings had opened a technical manual and hunched over the desk. His eyes moved around the page nervously, and his long, thin hands were clasped firmly between his legs as he leaned over the page. His lips were moving very slightly as he read. He could have been praying.

I remembered, just then, that on the Resolute there had been Norwegian chief "advisors" in the engine room as well as every other department. Hastings had been on the Resolute, I recalled, as a first engineer. When he came over with the rest of us he must have received a promotion as well. But on the Duchess we had only Hastings, and had always had Hastings, except when he went home for vacation. His relief was a very pleasant, witty engineer from Maine who for one reason or another I hadn't seen for a long time. When I asked Hastings about the lack of foreigners in the engine department he met my gaze with a faint smile of pride.

"It took a year. For a year on the Resolute I had to fight to convince the office that I was competent to maintain this ship myself. There was a trial period. You don't remember, I suppose."

I shook my head. I hadn't really paid much attention.

"It lasted months. We sailed from Seattle with two Norwegian chiefs. They stayed for sixteen weeks. In the end the chiefs admitted, and the office admitted, that I could do the job myself. I'm the only engineer in the company who has managed this." He practically beamed at me.

"Good for you... No, I mean it. What happened to the other guys? The Norwegians?"

He turned his palms up. "Went home? To where they belong?"

I was silent. Hastings. He smirked at me through his cleverness. Certainly he was a genius of some kind, but he reinforced my belief that technical brilliance has little to do with the evolution of human understanding. I couldn't resist a little needling in a way that might push his buttons.

"You remind me, in a certain way, of what I've read about Oppenheimer."

His eyes pushed at me. "I think I know what you are implying. I would suggest that you don't know enough about it."

"I know enough. I know what he stood for, what he urged our country to do. He was brilliant, like I suppose you must be in your field. But he lacked compassion."

Hastings jaw had set. He said, "You don't know anything about my capacity for compassion. I am a compassionate man."

"Maybe. But selectively."

He frowned. Pulled at his beard and picked up a pencil and toyed with it before placing it carefully beside his book. Then he said, "It would be an understatement to say that man has a wide range of points of view. The only way for any of us to get along is to accept the fact that every one of us are entitled to our own political beliefs. Whether you want to accept it or not, I am entitled to mine."

I said, "Of course you are. But it's when you act on them that shit blows up."

He scowled and returned to his manual. We didn't speak again until the fax arrived about a half hour later. I felt his eyes as I read it. When I looked up he said, "What's the matter?"

I swallowed. "Oh, it's my ex-wife. She needs more money."

He nodded briskly. I left. On the way up I felt a creepy leaden sensation in my gut as I read Nixie's brief message in my head again:

Painter: forty-two feet long

Tank: completely full

Gunnar had never left the ship. I was sure of that. And I was sure of something else -- that he was dead.

If we found the body, maybe we could figure out who killed him, and why. I had plenty of ideas. Too many, in fact. But now I had to bring the news to Taj. This was nothing I wanted to try alone. We had to form a plan of some kind.

But I didn't even make it to the deck shack.

13

The closest I ever came to getting killed on deck was in the late afternoon on a spectacular June day. One of those days at sea where the water lies still all around you and the ship glides across the surface like a stone on ice, so smooth and straight and true that you know there isn't a moment of doubt anywhere in the universe.

We were off the coast of Oregon, looking for what the fishmongers call pacific whiting but is actually hake. It is a slight, silvery fish about the size of an old coke bottle, vaguely phallic in form, and quick to decompose on the deck. The heat of the day was offset by a light breeze and the clouds were bright white and puffed and stretched loosely across the sky in every direction, casting mottled shadows across the rich blue of the sea. It was that time of day when if you stare unfocused at the water and let your mind go you see a hundred shades of lavender and violet among the reflections of the clouds.

It would have been as fine a time to die as any.

I was pushing a pile of rotted fish across the deck toward an open tank. The smooth and polished steel was hot under my feet and I had no thoughts but the brightness of the day and the fish and the heat of the deck beneath me.

The time had come for a haulback and the fishmaster stepped up to the panel and switched the controls from the deck to the bridge. In doing so he inadvertently released a seventy pound gilson hook that had been suspended high above the trawl deck. I was aware, for a millisecond, of a flash of movement in the corner of my eye before a force slammed into my head and sent me soaring sideways through the air. Moments like those happen outside our normal understanding of time. There is no sense of sequence of events. The seconds are compressed, but contain in them an eternity of violence.

I was wearing a thick plastic hardhat that shattered and landed in pieces several feet past my body. It was unusual that I had worn one on such a pleasant day, when fear of injury is far away and the last thing you want is a helmet strapped to your head. And I was the only one on deck who was wearing one. If my head had been bare it would have been smashed open like a ripe cantaloupe, brains and blood spilling across the deck like fish guts. As it was, strangely, I didn't have a scratch.

I got up seconds later, drained of color and shaking, and walked very slowly to the deck shack and sat down at the table. The room was cool and I sat and listened to the ring in my head. My saliva had a faint metallic taste. I sat there in the coolness and thought about life for a while and then I got up and returned to work. For the rest of the day and for a few days afterward I worked in a state of quiet reflection, pausing every once in a while to look around at the sea, at the birds, and the people around me.

When he hit me it was like that day in June except I wasn't wearing a hardhat. And it was not sunny and bright but bitter cold and windy and pitch black outside with a light snow blowing across the deck and sticking to everything like salt crystals after a low, low tide.

I had taken a shortcut through the raingear room and stepped outside into the wind and darkness near the skiff davit. I had taken maybe three steps when I saw a flicker and felt a force against my shoulder and neck that damn near took my head off. I flew six feet or so and slammed into the bulkhead and slid down onto the metal grating below. I looked up at the faint glow of the halogen lights aimed toward the trawl deck but Vidar's shape stepped above me and obscured even that light. He lifted me by the lapels of my coveralls like a sack of garbage and held me against the bulkhead for a second and peered into my wide eyes. A lit cigarette dangled from the corner of his mouth. Then he slammed me once, twice, and three times into the bulkhead and dropped me again to the grating.

He worked in a methodical silence that terrified me even through my shock, because I saw by his manner that he would be the agent of my death. He looked at me like I was a piece of net he had to untangle. He was rolling up his sleeves.

I started to say something but he grabbed me with his left hand around the throat and slowly pushed me up the bulkhead. He was speaking but I could barely hear through the ringing and the wind, and his accent was worse than ever. But I knew he was telling me to mind my own business. I wanted desperately to say what business -- was it the alcohol or the skiff or Gunnar or what -- but I couldn't formulate a word against the stone-like grip around my throat. In fact I couldn't draw a breath.

Then his right fist came like a truck into my abdomen and I saw a thousand points of light jump into the darkness. And then there was another and another and then nothing at all. Complete silence. No wind, no light, no breath.

Then I was aware of the warm and salty taste of blood in my mouth and the cold air rushing into my lungs and I opened my eyes to see the familiar oval shape of Taj's head above me. He was slapping me across the face and it felt good.

When he saw my eyes open he stopped and stared at me with his mouth half cocked and his eyes stretched in their sockets. I turned my head and little shocks of pain flew up through my neck to the base of my skull. I saw Vidar lying face down on the grating beside me, his hair wet and matted in a clump on the back of his head. Then I saw the long-handled shackle wrench lying between us.

My words were thick. "Chrimany, Taj, did you kill him?"

"Goddamn, Fish, I don't know, I don't know, but goddamm it what the fuck do you think you're doin? You trying to get yourself killed, motherfucker, and I swear if I killed this man here because of your gaddamned foolishness I might just kill you too."

He was upset, it seemed.

He turned Vidar over and put an ear near his face. Then he said, "You lucky, Fish. He breathin." He turned to me. "*Valea* ..." and then a phrase I couldn't make out.

I had nothing to say at the moment. Taj said, "What the hell he after your ass for, anyway? What did you do, what did you find out?"

I lay there without moving and told him about the skiff and my suspicions.

He said, "Yeah, well, maybe you're right about Gunnar, but I don't see why he have to be on the boat. If someone killed him, why not just drop him over the side?"

I shook my head. It hurt to do that. "No. Anyone smart enough to pull this whole thing off knows enough not to throw a body over the side of a boat pulling the biggest net in the world behind it. Chances are about even it'd go straight into the bag, then you got a body on the trawl deck and I think that's the last thing the killer wants."

"Who you think did it?"

"I don't know."

"Well, it look like you got a prime suspect right next to you."

I started to get up and Taj helped me. I was stiff and hurting and tasted blood but I didn't think anything was broken.

It took some effort to get the big man down the stairs and into the deck shack where we laid him on the long couch and placed a cushion behind his head. He wasn't bleeding too badly and Taj made a bandage and tucked behind the wound.

I gestured at Vidar and said, "I don't think this is about Gunnar. I think it's about what I did to the still in Hastings room."

"How you know that?"

"I'm not sure, but it doesn't fit. I just found out the news about the skiff fifteen minutes ago. We haven't seen Vidar all shift. In fact no one has. He wasn't in the wheelhouse when Alani was there, he wasn't in the engine room with Hastings. He's been almost comatose for days now. The only thing different that happened is that I ended his source of alcohol. I think he might have been hunting up some booze this shift and when he couldn't find it he got mad. At me."

"Which is understandable," said Taj without looking at me.

I nodded tiredly. "Big mistake on my part." I shrugged weakly, and said, "I was pissed off."

Taj ignored me, and poured us some coffee. Then he checked Vidar's breathing again. He said, "I'll see if he was askin' around. But you know Vidar don't know the processors too well. They ain't gonna give no bosun some booze maybe get 'em fired."

I stretched my neck a little. Felt like a chiropractic adjustment. "Is there a lot on the boat?"

Taj grinned. "Shit, Fish, you out of touch. This place is a regular speakeasy. I can get anything you want."

Vidar stirred a little. His eyes fluttered but didn't open, then a giant twisted finger jerked and lay still upon his chest. I looked at the bosun as I spoke to Taj. "How about you go find a bottle of whiskey?"

Taj stared at me for a moment, then gave a short laugh and disappeared into the night.

I saw that smashing the still had been a stupid thing to do. If Vidar was involved in Gunnar's disappearance, he needed to be kept under control. Alcohol, at least, had done a good job of that.

But even if he wasn't involved, it was still wrong to do, because it stepped over the line of what is acceptable, especially at sea. It's one thing to care for someone, but quite another to interfere with their business. Every man has a right to his own particular method of suicide. And on a boat with a hundred people, privacy is about all you have. The privacy of your thoughts, and of what you do to escape them.

But hell, I had no experience with drunks. My grandfather was the town drunk in a city in Ohio, but I never knew him. My father stayed pretty much away from it, probably in reaction to his childhood. As for me, I tend to have a few, laugh or cry a little, and go to bed. Vidar was something outside my experience. A force of nature that you kid yourself into believing you can control. If I was the Army Corps of Engineers, then lying before me was the Mississippi River. I wasn't sure if what I was about to do was right, but screw it, after the beating I had just taken, I was thinking mostly about survival.

Vidar opened his eyes and sat up and stared at me like I had just landed in something silver and shiny. He looked at me like that for a full minute until Taj returned and put a bottle of Black Velvet into his hands. He unscrewed the cap and as he slugged at the bottle he kept his eyes on me as if he were trying to achieve a reference point from which to begin to think.

Then I saw his memory return in bits and set itself in his eyes. But he didn't say a word. Not during the haulback nor anytime during the rest of the shift. In fact he didn't even look at me.

I had ceased to be a member of the set of things he considered worthy of his attention. A turn of events that at an earlier point in my career would have been cause for great regret, but which at that particular time was just fine by me.

14

We needed a body.

I was desperate to find Gunnar's corpse, if only to convince myself that I hadn't descended into a psychosis of paranoid delusion. The collage of inconsistencies surrounding Gunnar's disappearance had, for me, grown into a private world of mistrust and doubt, where I began to wonder about nearly every member of the key crew, and how each might benefit from the sudden departure of the old fishmaster.

Taj needed to find the body, if there was one, because it would bridge the growing gap of faith that had developed between us. The way he sometimes paused during a conversation, considering me for a moment in his smooth, laid-back way, as one might regard a close relative who had slipped a bit off the edge.

And he was right, as he usually was about most things. I had slid a bit off whatever edge I had walked on before. For the four days leading up to Vidar's assault I hadn't spent a moment in the social center of the boat -- the mess room -- instead retreating directly to Monique's chamber where the three of us created an isolated bubble of sensual delights and free-associated conversation. But each afternoon, when I showed up for work, and especially now, after the fax from Nixie, I had to face the doubts and dark fears about the people I worked among: Who was the killer? Or was there a killer at all?

After the haulback that evening we had five hours left in the shift. Taj and I decided that Gunnar was murdered or kidnapped between the hours of ten-thirty PM, when he went to bed sick, and about one-fifteen AM, when the processors would begin to get up for the two AM shift. It was during those two-and-a-half hours that the boat was at its most empty and silent.

I reasoned that the killer or killers would have had to transport Gunnar from his cabin to a hiding place where he would need to remain for a few weeks until the hold was full and we stopped fishing. Then, on the way into Dutch Harbor, without a net behind us, they could dump the body over the side without worry. During the same hours they hid Gunnar, they would have had to release the skiff from the boat. Given the two and a half hours, it was possible for the murderer to have dragged Gunnar to about any point on the ship with no trouble and still have time for the skiff. But the hiding place would have to be one in which the body could remain unmolested and not be subject to the ravages of decomposition. It also had to remain accessible.

That ruled out any of the heated cabins but opened up all of the frozen food storage areas, the coolers, any cool storerooms, the thousand ton hold itself, and the entire topside superstructure, which was guaranteed to be frozen for the next month. Or anywhere else, for that matter, where you might be able to store organic material to prevent decomposition.

We started on the bow, at the most forward point of the ship, in a small storeroom that was devoted to the storage of frozen goods for the galley. There was a hatch entryway from the bow itself, so we didn't have to disturb Tonni in the galley as he prepped the meals for the following day.

I opened up a box of frozen ribs. When I looked at the length of the bones he said, "You figurin somebody chopped him up, huh? Put him in these boxes, and we gonna eat him tomorrow, maybe?"

He was giving me that look again.

I shrugged, and mumbled something about thinking creatively.

Outside, the bow was mostly clear, except for a few icy snowdrifts along the railings which we poked at halfheartedly with broom handles. The bow was the darkest deck, since there were no overhead lights except the pale red, green and white lights on the mast. We tried to stay out of sight, close to the forward bulkhead below the wheelhouse, and if anyone from the bridge saw our shapes moving against the white background of the iced deck they made no mention of it. We could always say we were clearing the deck.

Taj pulled ice-covered pallets from piles of debris and tossed them over the side while I pushed at anything larger than a foot high, expecting at any moment to find the childlike form of the fishmaster curled up like a frozen fetus among tied bunches of floats and old bales of rotten web.

Taj said, "Bow need some serious cleanin."

"March," I said, "maybe April." I was cold, and my neck and guts still ached from Vidar's sledgehammer punches.

From the bow we could descend straight down a ladder through the thruster shaft to any level of the boat. At the bottom was the bow thruster room, where the sonar unit poked like a giant thermometer through a sealed, half-meter wide hole in the hull. Next to it was the bow thruster itself, really nothing more than a large thru-pump used to push or pull water back and forth across a cross section of the bow in order to better maneuver the large ship during docking.

But he wasn't there. Not floating in the pool of water encircling the globe-like bottom and shaft of the sonar unit. Nor wrapped around the base of the bow thruster, hog-tied with nylon rope and weighted beneath the surface with forty-pound trawl door shackles. I began to imagine him in these places, and tried to picture someone carrying the small lifeless form to some impossible crevice of the ship.

One level from the bottom was the freezer hold itself. This

area was the size of a warehouse, but I thought it unlikely because there was almost always someone down there; processors bundled in one-piece quilted suits, thick gloves and ski masks, stacking endless rows of sixty-pound boxes until they filled the fourteen hundred ton hold. Yet when Taj and I slipped down the far entrance and lost our breath to the thirty-below cold, there was no one there. There was usually a fifteen-minute to half hour lag time between stacking periods during the kind of fishing we were just then experiencing, so we rooted around for a half an hour among the stacks of folded cardboard boxes, plastic packing rolls, and boxes of frozen product. We found nothing.

Ice crystals had turned the outside fringes of Taj's slight mustache and eyebrows white, giving him a surreal devilish look. He said, "We reachin', down here, Fish. Ain't no way nobody gonna expect to take a body out of here after we done fishing. It'd be buried. Then in Dutch, durin the offload, processors down here movin boxes around and -- *hello, what's this*?" Taj shook his head. "I don't think so."

I didn't either. In fact, at that moment I remembered that Tonni and Steve had been down here, working with the groceries during our time-frame. I told Taj.

"Then what the hell we doin down here?"

I shrugged. "We were just leaving."

We passed through the lower surimi factory, where Japanese technicians milled about rows of control panels, and sprayed futuristic looking machinery with high pressure water hoses. We walked between a row of six layered and rotating cylindrical tubes, each a meter wide and thirty feet long. Screw presses. Snow-colored surimi paste pushed slowly through the outside layer of the tubes and fell into troughs filled with running freshwater. The search was turning slightly surreal in my mind. I tried to imagined Gunnar's small pale body converted and pressed into an off-white paste ... but no. Because the beginning stages of the surimi process had no capacity for objects larger than a pollock fillet. And once, years ago on the Resolute, when a wiseass processor had thrown a candy bar into a vat of surimi, it caused an uproar half a day later among the quality-minded Japanese. So Gunnar would have had to been gutted, flayed, deboned and chopped into tiny pieces to have fit into the works, there simply wasn't time nor place. And even if there was he never would have made it past the quality-control department.

When I voiced these thoughts aloud as we brushed by the factory, Taj gave me a look.

The upper factory held no secrets, since it was too warm to store a body and housed only fillet and mince machines. We passed the couple from Montana on machine number one and I heard them carrying on a conversation at the top of their lungs over the noise of the machine. Something about cattle, horses and wheat.

We checked the bilges on that level just in case, plunging

around the muck and blood of the bilge water, turning up fat floating codfish and sunken halibut but nothing else. We sat by the sorting area, where the fish were bled from the tanks onto stainless steel conveyor belts that ran them up to the fillet machines. The fish sorter, a frail tired-looking guy with a salt and pepper beard about forty-five years old that everyone called Sturge stood in a yellow hooded rain jacket and stared morosely at the fish as they passed. He rested with a hand on a hydraulic control and coughed a deep smoker's hack and ignored us as we sat there and talked.

Taj idly picked up a gaff hook and poked at the fish as they went by, occasionally spotting a cod or a jellyfish and flinging it onto the grating beneath the conveyor. Sturge nodded a slight gesture of appreciation for this simple favor and coughed some more. Everywhere the machines and conveyors screamed together and half the time I found myself reading my partner's lips.

"What about the engine room?" I shouted.

"Don't know nothin about the engine room."

"Neither do I."

"What?" he asked.

"Neither do I!"

We went down, not sure of where to look, and checked briefly behind boilers, under oil storage tanks. We stopped in the control room and talked to the oiler. Hastings was nowhere to be seen. Bob the oiler leaned with two hands against the desk, staring at a pressure gauge.

I said, "Hey Bob ... is there any dry ice on board?"

The oiler stared at me. "How's that different than wet ice?"

"Never mind."

We donned ear protectors and descended into the engine pit and I saw Hastings' wide brown shoes sticking out from under a roaring Wartsilla engine. We passed and then moved upward half a deck level into a series of small chambers devoted to various things -- a factory technician's workshop, a vented paint-storage area, an electrician's shop half the size of a closet where a compact bat-like man with huge ears and a flat face hunched over a circuit board with a voltmeter. I had never even seen the guy before, and wondered if people brought food and drink to the little room, but I saw no empty dishes. He barely glanced up as we entered and left a second later.

"Who the hell is that?" I asked Taj.

"New 'lectrician. Polish guy. Don't know his name yet."

"You've seen him before?"

Taj rolled his eyes. "You're the guy don't leave his room, Fish."

I couldn't resist a grin. "Would you?"

"Hah! Hell no, man."

We were running out of inside places to look and I was feeling doubtful about the superstructure. On the way to the deck shack we decided to pass through the sugar room and found Steve filling the bin with sugar. He pulled the mask from his face to reveal an expression of hope.

"Haulback, guys?"

We shook our heads.

I said, "How often you have to do this?"

"Almost never. I've been drivin' the fillet machine lately, but once in a while the Jap guy gets too busy to bother with it."

"You look happier these days."

He smiled. "Be even happier if we had a haulback."

The sugar room was hot and we left. I glanced into the nest and saw Vidar stretched out among the bags, cradling the empty bottle of Black Velvet in his sleep like a small child.

We took a break in the deck shack before going out into the weather. It was eleven. Three hours left that night to check the outside decks.

We started on the upper stern deck where the wind blew steadily from the port side. There was nowhere to hide up there, and the wind blew even through the metal grating that made up the deck itself -- the same grating my former partner had fallen through years before. Now it was covered completely with webbing and tied everywhere along the side to form a huge safety net.

We worked quickly to beat back the bitter weather, rearranging stacks of web, emptying bins of old chain and long, thick mooring lines. We even used the crane to lift three-ton bundled nets, but found only the desiccated carcasses of long-dead gulls and an occasional rat.

Taj and I went through every deck quickly and with the same attention to detail, but found nothing. It was one-thirty when we returned to the shack. I called the other shift for a wake-up and collapsed onto the cushioned couch. I was exhausted, every bruise and muscle ached, and I was discouraged as hell. Taj regarded me with a mixture of disappointment and pity.

"Well," he said, "it was a thought."

"It was."

In a way I was relieved. Now the question of Gunnar's death was in the hands of a higher power. I had done everything I could. If this was an ultimately just universe, which I continue to hope for, even now, then the matter would be resolved in ways that I didn't have to worry about. A cop-out, maybe, but you do what you can and leave the rest for fate.

Five minutes later we were was asleep on the two couches when Martin stepped into the shack.

"Where the hell have you guys been all night? I've been calling down here for the last two hours!."

I sat up. "Huh?" I yawned. Stretched. "Oh. we were out and about. Cleaning, mostly. Little tour of the factory. See what's going on. Why, what's wrong?"

"No big deal. I just need you guys to do something about the ice on the starboard side leading to the bow. I had to go up, shut a swinging hatch tonight and nearly broke my neck on the stairs."

"Shit, Martin. Sorry. I think we left the hatch open, too. We were just knocking some ice off, throwing a few pallets over. But we'll take care of it."

He leaned against the table and folded his arms. His eyes were red from the video screen and he seemed tired. "Yeah, I saw you guys earlier tonight. Wondering what you were doing up there in that weather. Anyway, if you can, get to it tonight."

"Okay. How's fishing?"

"Don't ask."

"Oh."

When he left Taj scowled. "We use up all our energy for the night chasin' your 'maginary corpse. Now we gotta go up with baseball bats, play ice ball.

"Nah. We'll just throw some salt down."

He looked doubtful. "That okay?"

I shrugged. All I could think about was bed. "Okay with me. Okay with you?"

"Ha ... you kidding?."

Taj got up and crawled into the sugar room. In less than a minute he was at the entrance again.

"We're out, *bra*."

"Out of what?"

"Salt. No more salt."

"Huh? How can that be? We had ten, fifteen bags leaving Dutch. We used one. Half a one."

"Fish, we're outta salt. Come see."

I went and saw. There was no one in the room but Vidar snoozing behind his wall of sugar bags. Taj stood on the port side of the room, where we had stacked separately the dozen or so bags of salt. Now it was just deck space, devoted partly to empty bags tied in compressed bundles with twine. There was no sign of any bags of salt, empty or full.

"It was just here four days ago. What the hell?"

"You tell me."

I looked around the room. Piles and piles of sugar bags. If someone was playing a strange game with stacking techniques it would take hours to uncover the bags of salt. But that made no sense. On the far wall were the sugar bins, and that's when I started to feel it: *Like thousands of bugs crawling on the inside of your stomach. Then they're fanning out, heading upward toward your lungs and downward into your guts. Down your arms now, through your groin. Paralyzed, and difficult to breathe.*

I stepped forward to the bin on the right, where the junk sugar was stored. It was piled high in a cone. I licked the tip of my index finger and touched the pile and a few hundred grains slid down like a microscopic avalanche. I touched my tongue. Just like licking a corn chip.

"Oh...shit," I whispered. I turned to face Taj and he was right with me. His eyes were like marble shooters.

Vidar's snoring sounded like a hurricane in the silence.

As I brushed the salt away in wide handfuls from the top of the pile it slid off and filled the creases of the sugar bags on the floor like snow.

The first thing to appear was the corner of a pair of eyeglasses. Then some skin, stretched sharp over the cheekbone, then the collapsed and crinkled eye socket itself, coated with a crusty brine. I stopped when I saw a nostril packed tightly with salt, and the first few locks of light grey hair.

We didn't speak at all as we returned the pile to the cone shape and dumped a bag of sugar on top for good measure. I checked a few places and the bin contained a mixture of both salt and sugar. That meant that occasionally Steve or the Japanese still used the bin to dump bad sugar. There was still plenty of room, and they could go on using it until the end of the trip. It was diabolically clever of someone, that was certain. The man was salted in the same way my Dad taught me to salt and then pickle herring from the cold April streams of New England where I grew up. The killer could leave Gunnar there indefinitely, counting on the general laziness of the crew, who had enough work to do without worrying about cleaning out spare bins full of what appeared to be useless sugar.

The deck shack clock showed fifteen minutes left in the shift.

I said, "What you think we should do?"

Taj paced around the room in small steps. "Shit, Fish, this ain't a cop show. And we ain't cops. We're suppose to tell the captain, I magine. Let him tell the Coast Guard. They come out, bust all our asses."

"They won't bust us."

"No, but they shut down this boat bout as quick as you can call it."

We listened to the clock tick.

"I don't think I want to tell the captain," I said. "I'm just not sure about him. Or anyone."

Taj was silent. He shrugged.

"I don't think I want to tell anybody right now."

"*Ta'ilo*. Whatever. Maybe we can figure out who did it. C'mon, Fish. We been talkin bout this for days like it was nothin. Dead body, no big deal. Like we a couple a badass detectives. But I didn't think it'd feel like this." Taj grabbed his own wrist to stop the slight tremor that had started in his left hand.

I made a quick, nervous smile. "Feels pretty strange."

"Feels good and bad at the same time. Scary as hell, but I feel like we got somethin important to do. Like a purpose. I say we find this *alelo* and bust their ass."

"So you're with me on this."

Taj looked at me. "Shit, *bra*. Where else I been?"

15

It was noon. We had agreed to wake up early to discuss things, come up with a plan. Taj sat across the table from me in the mess room, his eyes puffy and his face full of sleep. He wore a wrinkled hooded sweatshirt with a V torn into the crew neck to accommodate his thick neck. He stirred his coffee with an index finger.

"You look wonderful."

"Slept maybe one hour." His eyes scanned the mess room. We were off in a corner, there were two factory foremen taking a break from their shift on the far side of the room, otherwise we were alone. I heard Tonni clanging around in the galley behind us.

"Why?"

"Hah ... you kiddin right? Start callin you Shamus ..." He took a sip, made a face. "Na-sty *kae*."

"Norwegians like it strong," I said.

"Strong ain't bitter. When's that fat cook gonna learn that?"

"You're in a good mood, too."

"Lay up thinkin' all night. I'm one a them people don't have no pussy comin from six directions, calm me down."

I got up and got us a couple of pastries from the food line. In the galley Tonni was singing something I remembered from the Cowboy Junkies. He had a good voice.

When I sat down Taj said, "You take care a that ice last night 'fore we went to bed?"

"Sure. Can't let a little thing like murder keep us from our job."

Taj glanced around. "Shhh."

"They can't hear us. Look, I did something else, too. On my way up I had a thought about those gloves."

"Gloves, huh?"

"Yeah. If we can find out whose they are it might give us an idea about the skiff."

Taj shrugged. "How you gonna find that out? Could be anybody's. Maybe the guy borrowed 'em."

"I know. But it's a lead. You know, not everybody wears those kind. Deckhands ... I've seen the freezer crew with them sometimes."

We sat silently for a moment, then I asked, "Who else?"

Taj shrugged. "That's about it. They not that useful for most the jobs round here. Most the processors wear the long sleeve thin rubber gloves. These babies too thick for their line a work."

"Right. There's not too many floating around. So, what I did,

I brought 'em up to Alani last night. Turns out there's a little number on the inside by the wrist."

"Number? Like a serial number on a safety light?"

"Not exactly. A lot number. She writes down every purchase from the store, so Tonni can bill the customers, but she doesn't write down a number next to a name. Instead she just writes down the date she opens up a new lot. Does that on a separate piece of paper. For inventory."

"How many to a lot?"

"Twelve pairs."

I bit into a pastry. Tonni rumbled through the mess room and into the TV lounge with an empty tray. Thick white rolls of flesh encased in a T-shirt spilled from the sides of his apron and jiggled as he walked through the room. He was humming now and he smiled at me and winked as he passed by.

Taj said, "So how's she gonna connect a name with those gloves?"

When Tonni closed the door to the lounge I said, "She can't, but she can give me a list of the people who bought from that lot. She'll match the date she opened the lot and she'll write down everyone who bought that kind of glove until she hits twelve. Some of us buy more than one pair at a time. Sometimes I buy three at the beginning of the trip."

"You can afford it. I buy one, maybe two I'm feelin lucky."

"Well, what we'll have is a list of some people. If any of the names I have in mind comes up we might have something."

"This gonna take some time."

"She says she can do it tonight, after dinner. She has to open the store, anyway. People need their cigarettes. Hopefully she'll have some time."

Taj put his feet up on the opposite chair. He was looking a little better already. He said, "What names you got in mind?"

"Well, I'm trying to think motive. I mean, who'd have a reason to kill him?"

"Seems like a few people round here might want him dead."

I nodded. "We know about Hastings ..."

"That's one. How bout the cap'n? That man stepped right up an took charge like he was born for the job."

"I know. And I hate to say it ... God I hate to say it, but ... "

Taj said it instead. "Martin. Man's fishmaster now. I notice he give Jon control of the little things, but we both know who's runnin the fishin up there." He shook his head, and muttered, "O le va'a ua mafa tautai."

I smiled. That one I knew well. *This boat is full of captains...*

I said, "I can't believe he could do something like that. I've been thinking about it for days, and absolutely can't picture it but ... I mean, you think you know someone and then you find out you never knew them at all."

"'Specially up here."

"Yeah, but I golf with Martin at home. I've known him for

five years. He's the closest thing I have to a friend nowadays."

Taj shook his head. Drained his cup. I looked at the sea framed through the small round porthole behind his head. Rollers sailed past, crests breaking with a white rush of foam. Six days out now, and I didn't feel the motion of the ship unless I thought about it.

He said, "How bout the cook?"

I shrugged. "I've thought about it. Where's the motive? And can you picture him on that cable?"

Taj laughed shortly. "Be a sight to see. 'Sides, he was down that freezer, unloadin' pallets of groceries."

"Yeah, we gotta start placing these people. Hastings was on shift. But that doesn't mean he couldn't leave the engine room. Martin was fishing, but that doesn't mean anything either. The boat's on auto more often than not as it is. It's nothing for these guys to set a course and go down, have dinner."

"They ain't supposed to."

"I know. They usually don't. But they can if they want. I suppose Jon was in bed."

Taj was looking at me now carefully. He started to say something, then he stopped. That wasn't like him.

"What?"

"I wasn't gonna mention anything. Yet. But I will, I guess."

"What?"

"Last night I didn't just lay round the entire night. Couldn't sleep, got up, joined a little party they havin next door."

"The Idaho people?"

He laughed. "Those kids green, all right. Straight outta Boise. They good people, but they think a jellyfish somethin you put on toast in the mornin. But you wanna know some information bout who's doin who on the boat? *Kae*, Fish, that place is Gossip Central."

"I can imagine."

He cracked up now, smacked the table with a big hand, said, "Yeah, you a big topic a conversation over there ... but listen to this. One the girls, you know the little squeaky one, look like she maybe quit cheerleadin last week, but she still jumpin round squealin like she livin at a Bon Jovi concert?"

I pictured a cute, skinny blonde about five foot two with large breasts and a slightly upturned nose, lots of post adolescent energy. Wore one-piece, multicolored spandex outfits under her raingear. Drove the processing guys out of their minds. Made a lot of noise in the mess room with a table of friends, all of whom had big, big hair.

"Haven't got a clue to her name, but I can picture her."

"Well, her name don't matter. Fact, I don't know it either. But turns out she used to be a roommate with somebody sleepin with the cap'n."

"Jon?"

"Only cap'n we got. But check this out. Miss Cheerleader say this girl who sleepin with the cap'n was with him in his room the night Gunnar disappeared. Say the girl come back bout midnight that night. She remembered cause it was the last shift without fish."

"Midnight, huh? So there's two hours he was alone. Who's the girl?"

"That's the other part. That's what I wanted to wait on. See if there was a mistake, see if I could get some verification. But I don't think there's a mistake. Miss Cheerleader, she an expert on other people's business."

"What's to verify? We have to talk to the girl. You know her, Taj?"

"Well, I know who she is. But I think we gotta talk bout some things before we --"

"For Chrissakes, Taj, who is it?"

Taj shook his head. Paused, then said, "Monique, Fish. It's Monique."

16

It was almost as if she were waiting for me. It was one-thirty. Alani had gone to work. She sat cross-legged on the small half-couch in her cabin, dressed in a diaphanous little robe that lay open, framing her long torso in a pyramid of sheer cloth, exposing her breasts halfway across each nipple. Her eyes were closed when I first pushed open the door but snapped open and regarded me with clarity and brightness and with some amusement.

Through the glass behind her head I saw the wind blowing the tops off the waves in level rows of white sheeted spray. The sun shone beneath the clouds in heavenly rays against a stone-gray horizon.

Monique's smooth belly creased once below her breasts and the black triangle of her pubic mound showed itself above her crossed calves. I had a sudden desire to lay my head in her lap and feel her cool hands against the back of my neck and breathe deeply the rich smell I knew so well and that gave me such comfort. But instead I stood and we regarded each other for a moment before I leaned back on some cushions across the room and looked slightly up at her.

"Tell me about Jon Eliot."

She showed some surprise and her look of amusement deepened toward mirth. She leaned forward slightly and placed her chin on her first three fingers, then she leaned back again, clasped her hands and rested them where her ankles came together.

Her words were cool and light and measured.

"I know you, Fish, because you're very much like me. We're the kind of people that live alone most of the time in the privacy of our thoughts. This is true, isn't it?"

I shrugged. With Monique, I rarely felt that my thoughts were all that private, but I said, "Maybe.... But what about –"

She cut me off with her words, which came out a little sharper than usual, "Our idea of intimacy is not to connect with others in a meaty, kind of solid way, but to get just close enough to collect their stories. It's not such a bad thing, I guess, and it's nothing we can help. But have you ever thought about why we do it?"

I had no answer for her. She said, "I think we do it because our own stories are not alive enough for us, not as rich and deep as we think they should be, and we look for lives that are led closer to what we think of as real. Passionate lives."

It was probably true. She seemed to hold the world at bay with an intellectual aloofness which I suppose was achieved in my life by running away. Neither of us connected with the world in the way that most people did.

She said, "But when I go looking for passion from an empty place I almost always find darkness. What about you, Fish? Why are you with Alani and me? Is it to collect our stories, and then cast us away when you are bored with us?"

This is how Monique was. She spoke in a way that made you think she rehearsed her lines for an hour before you walked into the room. Of course she was right about me. I thought of my wife and daughter, and of friendships from my childhood in New England that had withered and died. And about the fact that I read literature to learn about relationships because it was safer than actually having them. But she and I and Alani had laid in the dark for hours talking about these kinds of things. I was impatient. I had little time and I needed some information.

"Monique, can we talk about us later? Right now it's important that I know about the captain."

She shrugged and smiled. "Of course it is."

I grasped her hands gently. "I'm sorry ... I just need to know - - were you with him the night Gunnar disappeared?"

She nodded in a nonchalant way. "I was. My own curiosity wants to know what you've seen that makes you look at me like that. But look ... you have to know that I couldn't care less about the crap that goes on in this silly little boat. I'll give you his story because I think that you're a good person, and I believe that what you'll do with it can do no more harm than what's already been done. Maybe later you can tell me what has happened.

I touched her hair, and took a deep breath, holding back my impatience. "Thank you. That's fair. But I can't say anything until I know more. I'm hoping you can help me."

"Maybe I can. The other night, the night you mentioned, was the last time I went to Jon. He has never asked me for anything other than to hold him like a mother would a small child. He would press his face against my chest, sometimes he would take my breast in his mouth and he'd cry. He'd cry for an hour sometimes.

"Maybe you know this ... but he's like a child. Emotionally, I mean. His father left when he was a baby. Left only him and a mother who started as a real estate salesperson, but then became rich by investing in La Jolla homes, and eventually mansions. But she was sick. And she married a man who was sick, too. He's only told me about one method of their abuse. I've never wanted to know more. Jon had a problem when he was a boy with wetting the bed. For punishment they would dress him in diapers and make him suck his thumb when his friends came over to play. They did this until he was nine.

"When he turned fifteen they sent him to boarding school in England. He had some problems, but they seemed to work themselves out and he managed to integrate himself enough to graduate. But his social success was on the surface. After high school he skipped college and moved to San Francisco where used his beautiful face to work for an escort agency. First it was women only, mostly older and wealthy, then couples, then men.

"But after a few years he gradually became less and less ... able to perform. He had to stop when he became impotent. He appealed to his parents for some money. By then they knew what he did for a living and they sent a letter saying that they would do one and only one thing for him -- send him to a school of his choice. Then he was never to bother them again.

"One day, he told me, he was standing near the base of the Golden Gate bridge on a foggy spring morning. He heard the blast of a horn and out of the mist came a huge ship leaving the harbor. As it passed he watched the tiny forms of men moving around on deck and the profiles of the masters in the house high above. They looked straight out toward a white wall of fog and didn't move as the ship disappeared altogether. He stared at the emptiness of the mist for a while and later that day he applied to the merchant marine academy. He shocked himself by succeeding at every turn there."

I tried to imagine the captain as a cadet, and found it pretty easy, considering he still looked like one. The boyish haircut, the smooth tan features must have carried him along. I said, "To be honest, he seems kinds of ... stupid."

She smiled. "He's pretending. He's actually brilliant. I'm not sure why he does it.

"Anyway, after a few years as a mate on cruise ships and tankers, he sat for the masters license and passed. Last year he took the job in Seattle because of the money and because, he told me, he liked the city.

"He's never been married, and he tends to attract people who have very strong maternal or paternal instincts. He's loveable in a terribly innocent way, but I imagine that he can't have a relationship because he's not an adult in any sense of the word. In Seattle he calls up a service that sends a woman who dresses him in diapers and holds him while he cries."

I said, "A woman --" and she nodded and I knew. "You're a call-girl? That's how you met him? Is that how you came up here?"

She smiled briefly. "Definitions. We think we are so good at them. I'm a specialist, I guess you could say. I work for a service that caters to a certain kind of individual. Sometimes I dress people in diapers. Sometimes I do other things, but all in keeping with my own nature. In this way I try to stay true to myself. I like to think that I what I do keeps a certain kind of person from descending into a place that they can't escape."

"My God, Monique, you must be aware of the danger."

She pulled her robe together against a chill that had entered the room. "Yes. It's not something I'll do for long, I think." She smiled suddenly. "In fact, I'm done! Meeting Alani and you was like stepping into a pool of sunlight."

"Mmm. Especially Alani. Maybe in some ways I am like you but Alani is nothing like either of us."

She nodded. "She wants to go to a sunny place after all this.

Not realizing that she herself is a ray of sunlight. I'll follow her anywhere."

"Why hasn't Jon come to you again? Did you come up in a ..."

"Professional capacity?" She laughed. "No. Jon arranged the job for me but he has never asked anything of me other than an occasional comfort. Never for money. Only because he was in pain. And I think he stopped when he saw what was happening between the three of us."

"He's grown in ways, hasn't he, since Gunnar has disappeared?"

She said, "He has. He was forced into a leadership position. For the first time in his life he had to run a ship. But are you implying that he had something to do with Gunnar's disappearance?"

"I'm not implying anything."

"Because I don't think so. I don't think he's capable of violence."

"How do you know what anyone is capable of?" I said.

"Because I've had experience with different kinds of sickness. I can sense when someone is on an edge -- that kind of edge. I've never felt that Jon has reached that point. His is a sickness of emptiness. He was never loved as a child." She looked down and toyed with the corner of her robe. She said, "But I'm not a psychologist. I could be wrong ... but I don't think so."

"What was he like when you left him that night?"

"Oh ... he had cried for an hour or so. He was tired, and happy in a peaceful way that he gets before he goes to sleep."

"What do you think he did after you left?"

"I think he probably went to sleep."

It was five minutes to two.   I stood up and took her chin in my hands and kissed her on the lips. She smiled shyly and I saw an expression I hadn't seen in her face before. "You don't think less of me, knowing this?"

"Monique, you are the most beautiful and interesting woman I've ever met. In every way. And inasmuch as I'm capable of it, I love you. You don't need my approval. You know that."

She nodded and there were tears in her eyes. We held each other and listened to the wind until I left for work.

17

What a mess the deck was.

Bjorn's shift had wound the net halfway onto the reel and left the rest trailing into the water like a black stocking the length of a football field. At the end of the stern they had bunched the net and had wrapped it with a length of chain that they fastened to a thick steel rail. This stopped the net from slacking further into the ocean while they eased more net off the drum. By the time I slipped on my deck suit and stepped out of the shack, Vidar, Taj and Steve were already there along with the four guys from the other shift. Bjorn had spread a section of the net around the deck like a giant blanket, and deckhands were stationed at various places throughout like flies caught in a spider web. Major project.

The word was that Jon had more or less played chicken with the fishmaster on the Kodiak Venture, and lost. The Kodiak wouldn't admit it, of course, but the their trawl door had taken away a piece of our net about the size of a stadium parking lot. But it wasn't their fault. It's up to our captain to maintain some contact with oncoming boats, especially when they're oncoming from the starboard side. If that's case, as it was with the Kodiak, it's up to us to move. Which we didn't. Or at least not enough.

I approached Rusty, who was holding a handful of twenty-foot meshes straight while Bjorn worked furiously with a twine needle the size of a baseball bat. I moved to take the meshes from him but he shook his head.

"We're all stayin, Fish. Least 'til it's done."

I could see their point. From the way it looked, the hole would take a while to repair.

"How much time you guys got invested so far?"

Rusty said, "Six hours. Happened, what, Bjorn -- 'bout eight-thirty?"

Bjorn nodded and smiled, his odd mustache curling upward. "Yes. Just after Martin handed Jon the controls and went to dinner. Hah!" He pronounced the captain's name "Yahn."

I glanced upward and saw both men standing at the window of the wheelhouse. Jon looking worried, Martin looking merely grim and he watched the work with his hands in the back of his pockets. Time, as always, was money, and by the look on his face we were losing a lot of both.

Vidar was sewing next to Bjorn. I watched the master at work. The hardest part was to get the net straight enough to sew. It's one thing when the meshes are the length of your index finger. Then they line up in a nice, neat row. But when each diamond-shaped mesh is as long as an Olds 88, it gets interesting.

Vidar yelled, "Needle!" and Steve fell all over himself to locate another long plastic net needle loaded with twine. Bjorn took it from his hands and the two bosuns spoke in their language for a moment and laughed loudly. Steve stared at them, then me, suddenly angry. I saw the question in his eyes. They laughin' at me?

Probably, I would have said.

Over the years I had worked with some Norwegian bosuns who barely spoke to their American deckhands. When they were forced to say something, it was always with a gruff backhand manner that was tough to take if you had any self respect. I saw a lot of potential talent driven off the deck because they couldn't stand the cultural elitism and tyrannical nature of certain bosuns. Vidar wasn't too bad, but he had his moments. I suppose this is a tradition in Norway. Every bosun has a story about the old country that features an ogre for a deck boss. This is to make you think that they're being charitable in comparison. Maybe they are, but it's hard for some Americans to take this kind of thing from foreigners. I never had a problem, but for a few days I had been seeing a subtle change in attitude in our boy Steve.

I looked across the net. Steve stared with a set jaw at the meshes in his hand. Vidar worked calmly before him, oblivious to his mood. The other deckhands looked merely bored.

I said, "Steve, come and help me for a minute in the shack,

will you?"

He handed the meshes to Taj, who stood next to him. Now Taj stood holding two sets straight out from his sides like an anatomy study by Leonardo. Steve followed me into the shack.

"I figure we'll get ahead of these guys. Fill some needles in here. It's warmer, anyway."

He nodded, took his helmet off and set it on the table. He sat down and picked up a spool from the floor and started wrapping the twine around a long, flat plastic needle. He had big hands that were red from the cold. His suit was barely soiled and he carried two knives strapped to his waist and one around his shoulder in a kind of sling he had made. Like most newbies, he looked like he was on a commando mission.

I said, "What's up, Steve? You look a little pissed off."

He looked at me. His blue eyes were hard and his lips a thin line. "What were those guys laughin at out there?"

I chuckled a little. "Shit, Steve. You can't be worryin about such things. Probably laughing at the memory of some drunken night in Greenland six years ago."

"It's not just that, Fish. I've been working my ass off out here for more than a week. You'd think Vidar would look at me once in a while. Maybe say something."

"Ah, you know Vidar. He doesn't even talk to me anymore. But I know where you're comin from, man. You'd like a little recognition from someone who counts, instead of just me and Taj, right?"

He blushed a little. "It's not that."

"Bullshit. It is that. I had to go through the same thing, but worse. Listen, you aren't gonna get anything from these guys. Not for a long time. That's just not the way they operate. It's a different culture. But they have a point, too. They don't want anybody's head blowing up so much they can't put on their hardhat, you know what I mean?"

"Yeah. But Bjorn looks okay."

"Bjorn's a nice person, from what I've heard. A lot of these guys are easy to work with. When Martin was the deck boss on the Resolute, the job was a party. But it's not always gonna be like that. But you can learn more from watching Vidar, even if he is a pain in the ass, than you can from anyone."

"Bjorn's good too."

I sighed. "'Course he is. But the grass isn't always greener. You want to switch shifts, it's up to you. But it's a little early in your career."

"Uh huh." He looked down at his work.

"Somethin else bothering you, Steve?"

He looked up quickly. "No. What do you mean?"

"Oh, I don't know. Just seems like you've had somethin on your mind these last few days, is all."

"This have to be some kind of personality contest, Fish? I need to be happy and cheerful to be a good deckhand, or what?"

I stood up without looking at him and moved for the door.

He said, "Hey, man I didn't --" but I was on the deck and not listening. I figured that either the kid would work things out or he wouldn't. At that point it was my view that Steve's problem had little to do with me. Of course I was wrong. Maybe someday someone will invent a computer program that corrects our most important blunders in advance. That'd be a nice thing to have.

I hate freak accidents. I hate the concept, I hate the words themselves -- "freak accident" -- as if some strange beast was responsible instead of the normal workings of fate.

I mean it's one thing when a guy does something he's not supposed to do. I've seen deckhands resting their hands on the stern roller during a haulback. Or absently pushing a leg against the net as it whips by on the way out. And even standing with their stupid face leaning two feet into the bight of a slackened wire.

I'm not unfeeling enough to say that these men deserved what they got, but it was understandable when it happened. You could look at the aftermath and say, "*now that could have been prevented.*"

But what happened that night -- I mean, you believe in a just and loving God and see something like that, your faith goes right out the window.

The net was finally finished at eight-thirty. By then it was cold and dark. Bjorn and his crew had left when the hole became manageable with just four of us. That was about five o clock. Now we were ready to shoot the net, and all I could think about after six hours of standing around holding meshes like an idiot was to get into the shack and warm up.

It was impossible to see past the lights and into the wheelhouse but whoever ran the controls was in more of a hurry than even I was. He was slacking full speed on the drum and only stopped after I jumped up and down for the fourth time screaming and waving my arms. I had stopped him because the net had backlashed, but now it was a disaster. I ran up to the drum and started yanking at the caught meshes and was joined by Steve. Taj and Vidar stayed in the back and gave hand signals to the bridge to move the drum back and forth. It was then that the hydraulic power stopped. First I heard the hydraulic motors winding down in the room off the port side, then the drum itself slowed to a stop.

Vidar cursed and left the deck. It looked like he was heading for the engine room. I told Steve to keep working at the backlash and I stepped into the room that housed the hydraulic motors. Taj stayed where he was on the deck, shielding his eyes against the halogen lights, trying to see into the wheelhouse. Inside the room I approached the closest pump, which stood high and round and silent on a pedestal like a Mayan tablet. But before I took three steps it kicked on suddenly, along with the rest of them. I remember I shrugged and turned to face the doorway and from the darkened room I saw the net speeding inward toward the drum. A picture of Steve flashed in my mind and I ran to the doorway and began to shout but it was too late. I heard Taj's screams in the background and saw Steve's suit, bright red in the halogen lights, spinning around and around on the drum, each time covered by another layer of the net.

All at once the drum stopped dead. I looked around for Vidar but he hadn't returned from the engine room. Pictures flashed through my mind from the thousand times I'd seen sharks and octopus caught in the net the same way, their body parts falling onto the deck in great chunks. I felt dizzy. When I got to the drum, Taj was already there, hacking away at the layers of black netting that covered Steve's form. Blood dripped from where I supposed the combi's face was under the web. Taj was making strange noises from the back of his throat as he worked. Steve's helmet lay beneath the drum and rolled around with the motion of the boat.

I said, "Forget it, Taj. Let me go to the bridge and slack this off. I don't know what the fuck is going on, but I'll find out. Watch for me. Give me signals."

He nodded. I took the entrance near the galley because it was closer to the net reel. As I ran through the mess room I saw Tonni entering from the other side. Martin sat at a table and said, "What's wrong?" as I passed but I didn't answer.

Tonni said, "Fish, if you see Jon could you tell him --" but I ran past him too and up toward the bridge. When I reached the wheelhouse it was empty. Through the front window I saw Jon on the bow. He was on the very top of the mast, dressed in a deck suit. He was changing the front fishing light. What the hell?

I stood at the control panel and waved at Taj but he couldn't see me. I started to slack the drum slowly and he jumped forward and stood under the drum. I saw Vidar appear behind him and then I saw his shock as he drew closer. Then Vidar stepped back and guided me the rest of the way until the twisted body of Steve fell into Taj's arms like a doll made from a stuffed monkey.

I was in a state of confusion when Martin appeared at my side. I had begun to wind up the net and he said, "What's going on? What are you doing? Where's Jon?"

I didn't look at him. I said, "We're going to Dutch."

"What? What the --"

I said, "Look!" and pointed downward at the drum. He had to crane his neck to see Vidar and Taj bent over the lifeless form of Steve.

"My God, Fish, what happened?"

I stopped with the drum and stared at him. I said, "How long have you been eating?"

He started with "What has --" then he saw my face and said, "Twenty minutes. Why?"

I heard the hatch to the bow open and Jon stepped in. His cheeks were red from the cold and he whistled as he shucked of his suit. He said, "Guys done with the net yet?"

Martin was still looking at me but I had turned to face Jon. I was still confused. "Jon, how long have you been out there?"

He shrugged. "Five, ten minutes? While you guys were working on the net I noticed the fishing light was out. I thought I'd change it myself, you guys being busy and all." He smiled and joined us at the console.

I said, "Let me get this straight. You, Martin, have been eating for twenty minutes and you, Jon, didn't even know we were done with the net? Weren't either of you just up here slacking the goddamned thing out full speed until I jumped up and down like a maniac to stop you?"

Jon stared at me. "What the hell are you talki--"

"Answer the fucking question!"

Jon said "Listen, mister I don't--"

Martin touched his shoulder and said, "Hold it, Jon." He said to me, "Fish, calm down. I don't know what's going on, but why don't you start from the beginning. Maybe we can figure this out."

I stared at both men before me. I was suddenly gripped by a feeling of unreality. I needed to get away from them. I said, "I'm going down. We can talk about it later. I'd get the net in if I were you."

Martin said, "Wait, Fish. Tell me --"

But I was already out the door. As I shut the hatch I heard Jon starting with, "What the --"

When I reached the deck I was amazed to find that Steve was

still alive. He lay in a pool of bloody ice water on the deck, eyes closed and barely breathing. I helped Taj and Vidar lift his broken body onto an aluminum stretcher. In less than a minute Jon came running down the steps from the wheelhouse.

The captain took control of the situation, directing us into the accommodation where we set the stretcher on the floor of the raingear room. Taj used a folded sweatshirt to dab at a thin trickle of blood from the corner of the Steve's mouth. It was impossible to tell how many bones were crushed through the deck suit but by the way his body twisted in the stretcher I knew he would never be the same again, if indeed he lived. I heard the winch reeling the net onto the drum. Vidar stepped out onto the deck.

I look across at Jon. "Dutch?"

He nodded. "Full speed, as soon as we get the net in."

"How far are we?"

"A day. Day and a half. I'm not sure."

"Wow."

"Mind telling me what happened?" asked the captain.

I said, "Taj, can you tell him? I'll help Vidar get the net in."

I left the raingear room and joined Vidar. We worked in silence, without looking at each other. That was fine. My mind was racing for a solution. I replayed the sequence of events: net slacking full speed, backlash, hydraulic power out, Steve under the drum, probably hanging from a mesh, then full speed hauling. Where was everyone? Martin said he was eating the whole time.

Jon said he wasn't in the wheelhouse, and he was changing the bulb when I went up after the accident. Either someone one was lying or someone else was up there, running the controls.

Vidar was just a few feet from me now, holding the other end of a rope. I said, "Was Hastings in the engine room when you just were there?"

He shook his head. He said, "Just a boy."

"Why were you gone so long?", I asked, not thinking how it might have come out.

His eyes looked like blue ice. "Looking for the chief."

"It's possible, isn't it, to turn off the hydraulics from the bridge?"

He nodded but I knew the answer anyway. There were three places on the ship from which you could control the hydraulic pumps. The pump room on the port side of the trawl deck, the engine room, and the bridge. Someone could have been in the wheelhouse and completed the whole process. But it didn't make sense. Why kill the combi?

Unless they weren't trying for Steve at all. It was difficult to tell any of us apart at night, especially when we wore the same type of suits. Whoever it was could have been trying to kill me.

When the net was on the drum I returned to the raingear room to find Tonni leaning over the stretcher. Tears were running down his cheeks and he rocked back and forth on his knees and made a high- pitched wailing noise. I remembered then that the boy was a relation of some kind. Behind him I saw the captain discussing something with Hastings, who stood with his back to Tonni. His face was chalk-white and he licked his lips often.

I said, "Can you explain this, Hastings?"

He looked baffled. He said, "This is horrible. I've never... I've not seen an injury like this before."

I saw Taj watching him intently from a few feet away. I said, "I mean can you explain what might have happened with the pumps? You know they went off and --"

"Yes. The captain has told me. The only possible explanation is a problem with the wiring." He raised his arms, palms up. "Maybe a short shut the pumps off, then turned them on again."

"Then heaved up the net full speed?" I said.

He shrugged. "It's possible. It's very unlikely, but it is possible. If it happened, it'd be the first time I've ever heard of such a thing."

"A freak accident, then?"

"Yes. A freak accident."

Jon was watching me as I spoke. He said, "Paul, there's bound to be an investigation about this no matter what happens to Steve. We're on our way to Dutch Harbor right now. I know you're upset, but maybe it's best you give it a rest, okay?"

"No problem." I looked at Tonni. He was quiet now and rested a meaty hand on Steve's forehead. The kid's face looked small and soft and pale in the neon light from the room.

I said to Jon, "You want to move him?"

"Yes. Tonni says there's an empty room just inside."

Inside the cabin we set the stretcher onto the lowest bunk and tied it to the bed frame. Jon left immediately to call for medical advice and Tonni returned from the galley with some damp towels. I nodded to Taj and we started for the door.

Tonni said, "You boys did everything you could. Thank you."

We left him and headed back to the deck. My mind was still racing. I tried to think about what Hastings said. It seemed like it had to either be a conspiracy or a crazy electrical accident like Hastings said. None of it made sense. A conspiracy? I wondered if I was getting paranoid, but then that was what I thought before we found Gunnar's body. Chrimany, there was still that to think about. I had about decided to call it an accident in my mind until I could prove otherwise when we ran into Alani at the foot of the stairs leading to the galley. She had heard about the injury.

She said, "Fish, how bad is it?"

"Bad."

She was pale and trembling. "Is he going to die?"

I held her. Taj put a hand on my shoulder and stepped out onto the deck. "I don't know, babe. He might."

"Oh, no. Fish, I feel horrible saying this but I just thank God it wasn't you."

"I know. Every time something like this happens I feel just as bad for thinking the same thing."

Chapter 17

"Fish, please quit this life. Come away with us."

Her sweet face looked up at me. I said, "I don't know what I'm going to do, Alani. Right now I just want to figure out what's going on. Oh yeah, did you get that list of names?"

"Uh huh ... right here." She dug a small piece of yellow lined paper from the pocket of her jeans. I opened it and read a list of six names. I was the first, then Taj, then three freezer guys, but the last name turned my guts to jelly. The name was Stephen Girard.

18

Taj and I were outside, sitting on the dry cod end piled on the starboard side, when the captain came to tell us that Steve had died. It was less than an hour after we had brought the stretcher into the room. The sea had roughened up a bit and without a net in the water the boat rode high on the waves. We were heading toward Dutch Harbor at fifteen knots. I had just finished telling Taj about the gloves. The captain stood with his hands in the pockets of a lined jacket, bracing himself against a sharp wind. His blonde hair blew back as he spoke to us.

He said that Tonni had called him, hysterical over the intercom, just ten minutes after Taj and I had left the cabin. Tonni told him the boy had simply stopped breathing. Jon tried CPR for a half hour and couldn't get a pulse, so he gave up. The captain told us he had given Tonni some tranquilizers and sent him to bed. Jon's eyes had begun to water from the cold and he shivered. He said he was going back up to report the death to the Coast Guard. We watched him take the steps back to the wheelhouse two at a time.

Taj said, "Man should be reportin' two murders."

I was absently tying knots in the chafing gear, thinking. Before the captain came down we had been discussing Steve and the gloves and Gunnar, trying to make connections.

I said, "I should have pushed the kid today. Something was bothering him, he wouldn't tell me. Like an idiot, I just walked away from it."

"How was you s'pose to know? You think he killed Gunnar?"

"I doubt it. No reason. He barely knew the old man. But he must have been involved somehow, and it cost him his life."

"Then you don't buy that stuff from Hastings bout the electronics."

I shook my head. "Hell, no. But the thing is, the guy seemed completely spooked. He looked sincere. Like he believed it himself."

"I know it. Could be, he scared of something else. Or somebody else. Maybe we oughta talk to the man."

"Not yet. I don't want to get too close. We have another problem."

"What's that?"

I watched the cloud of my breath rise in front of me for a moment. I glanced into the deck shack and said, "Where's Vidar?"

Taj grinned. "I hooked him up with the freezer guys yesterday. He their best customer now. He the problem you talkin about?"

"No. It's that we're done fishing now. No more net in the water.

If Gunnar's body is going over the side, it'll happen in the next in the next twenty-four hours."

Taj's eyes widened. "What you want to do?"

"What's happening down in the factory?"

"They got about five hours worth of fish left. Then they'll be cleanin for twelve or so."

"So it's crowded down there. No way the killer can take the body through the factory. He'll have to use the deck shack."

"Not so long as we're here. But what we gonna do, hang around all night, all day tomorrow?"

"We could. But there's another idea."

"Yeah?"

"Yeah. We force his hand. Give him a reason to come in the next few hours."

"How we gonna do that?"

I told him. He thought it was a crazy idea, but one that might work.

When I was a little kid and things got so knotted up inside I couldn't think, or when I feel like my back was against the wall, it seemed like my mother was always around to smooth out the creases, explain the world. Dad was there too, but we had a different kind of relationship. I rarely took problems to him, because I wanted to be sure and strong around him, as he always was around me. When I got married, life became even more complex, but then I had a wife to help me think things out, and I suppose she took on the role, at times, of a surrogate mother. So it was no surprise that I thought of calling Stephanie now. Half of it was, I think, that I just wanted to hear her voice. But I also needed a contact on land I could trust, and she was it.

It was eleven PM in Seattle. I used the satellite phone in the hallway above the raingear room. It was fairly quiet, just a couple of foremen passed, returning from a break in the mess room.

I dialed the number and got the Marisat operator. It would be collect at ten bucks a minute, but I knew Stephanie would accept the charges. Sometimes it pays not to be a deadbeat.

Her voice crackled through the line. "Paul? Paul?" She had stopped calling me by the nickname when we were divorced.

"Hey, Steph. How's Ellany?"

"Hi. She's great. Just fine. She's asleep. She had a big day. We took her to the zoo."

We.

"That's great, Steph."

"It was fun. I guess you got the message I sent."

"What message?"

"Oh ..." she sounded confused. "I thought that's why you called. I left a message at your office for you to call. I have some news."

"News?"

"Yes. Some wonderful news. Paul, I'm getting married." Even

through the lousy connection her voice sounded full of happiness.

"Paul? Are you there?"

"I'm here."

"Did you get that? Did you hear what I said?"

"I heard. That's ... great, Steph."

"You're upset, Paul. I can hear it. I knew you'd be upset. Please ..."

"We can talk about it when I get home, Steph."

"I'll be married when you get home." I was hating the way she said that word.

I pressed the receiver into my ear until it hurt.

I said, "What?"

"The wedding is in two weeks. Paul, you have no reason to be upset. It's not fair. Don't try to spoil this for me."

"How long have you known this guy?"

"Don't be stupid, Paul. It's Randy. You've met him."

"Oh. The lawyer."

"Yes. The lawyer. I don't like the tone of your voice. I hope you're not going to be difficult about this."

"I won't." And I wouldn't. I had no right, anyone would agree to that. I had made my decision years ago, and I knew that this day would come. Right? So why was I feeling like the ground had opened up beneath me and I falling straight down to the Big Nowhere?

"Paul ... if you didn't get my message, why did you call? Is everything all right?"

"Everything's fine, Steph. I just need you to do a favor."

"Anything, love."

"Please don't call me that, Steph."

"I'm sorry. You know I still love you."

"Steph, I need you to send a fax. Two, actually. To the boat."

"Okay. I'll get a pen." I heard her set the phone down. I heard a man's voice in the background. The lawyer.

"Okay Paul." I dictated as she wrote. When I was finished, she said, "Paul, what is this about? Who is this 'Gunnar'? Is this a practical joke?"

"Yeah. That's what it is, Steph. You know how things are up here. Bunch a guys, having a blast."

"Well, it's an expensive joke."

"Listen, Steph. This is pretty important. I need you to send this right away."

"Paul, it's eleven o clock."

"There's a KINKO's on second avenue downtown. Send it from there. Send one each to the two numbers I gave you. But you can't use their cover sheets. Send only this message and make it look as legit as you can. Look, if you can do this one thing, I'll never ask you for anything again."

"Oh, for God's sake, Paul, it's not that big a deal. Of course I'll do it."

"Thanks, Steph. And Steph?"

"Yes?"

"Say hello to Randy for me. Tell him congratulations."

"Okay, Paul. I love you."

"Bye, Steph."

After I hung up it took minutes to climb up to the wheelhouse roof where the cluster of antennae and spinning radar beacons stood against the black of the night sky. Directly above the radio room I found two sets of steel boxes under two sets of antennae. It was the satellite receivers/transmitters for each of the separate fax and phone lines. I identified the phone system and ripped out every wire leading in or out of the box. Crude, but hell, I'm not an electrician. The important thing had been accomplished: there would be no more phone calls that evening.

19

There was nothing to do but wait. There was no outside reason for us to go anywhere or do anything. The fishing was finished until we returned to sea, and as far as I was concerned, if there was some cleaning to do, it could wait for the other shift. Once the faxes arrived, I felt the killer or killers would move immediately. It was ten-twenty when I hung up with my ex-wife, and I expected something to happen within three hours. Stephanie was sending a phony emergency message from the Operations Director of Northern Seafood's to both the wheelhouse and the engine room. The letter explained that the Coast Guard had found the body of an old man washed up at St. Paul and that it looked like a homicide. The Coast Guard was flying the corpse to Dutch Harbor and the crew was ordered to head in to identify the body and, if it turned out to be Gunnar's, submit to an investigation.

I knew the fax would stir something up. If there was more than one person responsible for Gunnar's death, maybe one would think the other had panicked and thrown the body overboard. There'd be no way to verify the fax by calling the director, since the phone was dead. In any event, I knew that someone would likely show up to check on the body.

We stationed ourselves in the doorway of the sugar room at the back of the deck shack. From there we could see both the entire room as well as the laddered entrance from the factory. With both exits covered, no one was getting near the second sugar bin without our notice.

We waited. Taj played with the solid steel bar he had brought with us, 'just in case', he had said. We tossed around some ideas, but came to no definite conclusions. There were too many loose ends flying around. I had some strong ideas but I decided it was best not to get trapped in one way of thinking about it. I favored the method of flushing someone out and leaning on them until we had some answers.

Taj brought up the point that in order for anyone to dispose of the body, they could have to dispose of us, as well.

"Think we can handle them?" I asked.

"Shit, depends on who they are. If it turn out to be Vidar and he shows up sober, pissed off and with some help, I guess we in for some trouble."

"What makes you think Vidar?" I asked.

"Only connection I can see to Steve. They worked together. All the times they were over there on the other side they coulda been talkin' 'bout all kinds a things."

"Steve told me just today that Vidar never talked to him. It always seemed like Vidar ignored the guy."

"All the more reason."

"I suppose," I said.

We waited some more. And as I sat there turning some things over in my mind I came across a nasty enough thought to send me to the intercom where I dialed the number to the laundry room. Alani answered.

"Hey, babe."

"Hey, Fish. Is everything okay? How is Steve?"

"Steve's not doing so well, Alani. In fact, nothing is really okay. Can you do me a favor?"

"Sure."

"Could you go to Monique's room and lock yourselves in and don't come to the door unless it's me."

"What? Fish, I'm at work. I can't--"

"Alani, sweetheart, this is really important. Please do this. Take the rest of the night off. I can't tell you why right now, but trust me, there's a good reason. If there's any problem, I'll talk to whoever I have to in the morning. Okay?"

Nothing came over the intercom for a half a minute and I was heading for the doorway when I heard her say, "Okay, Fish. After I put in this load."

"Now, Alani. Please."

"O-*kay* already."

Taj gratefully accepted the coffee I brought back with me. He had overheard the conversation.

"Way to cover those bases, brutha."

"I just want one less things to worry about. But damn, Taj, half the time I don't know whether I'm being cautious or paranoid."

"No such thing as paranoid when you're dealin with shit like this. You saw what Steve looked like after he dropped off that reel. These people a little dangerous, I think."

After about twenty minutes I called Monique's cabin. Both her and Alani were there and they demanded to know what was going on, but I managed to hold them off with the promise that I'd be there by three AM and explain everything. There was a chance that it could be a lie, that I wouldn't be there at all, but I wasn't about to let them know that.

When the intercom buzzed at one AM it snapped me out of a reverie that was leading to all kind of strange places. It was Martin.

"Vidar! Fish!" he shouted through the intercom.

"Vidar's not here! What's up?" I moved closer to the monitor.

"There's a fire in one of the storerooms below the bow! Just off the galley. Get your asses up there and get some fire hoses ready. I'll meet you." He hung up.

I looked at Taj. "This is it, man. You ready?"

He was shaking his head coolly, but I could see what was underneath. He said, "Shit, these some clever bastards. What you wanna do?"

"You take off. Go on up, fight the stupid fire. I'll stay here, take care of this."

"You crazy?"

"Go, goddammit, one of us has to show up there. Don't worry about it. I know who's coming. I think I can handle 'em."

"You know? How--"

"Just go! Leave me this bar. *Go!*".

He went. I took the bar and crouched down behind a pile of empty sugar bags that were stacked along the wall closest to the deck shack. If they came in from the factory, I'd be across the room, if they came through the deck shack, I'd watch them walk by three feet away.

Blood pounded in my head and chest like hammers and my stomach was knotted like a nasty backlash. Breathe ... breathe ... breathe.

What a fucking amateur, I was thinking to myself.

20

When Vidar entered the room from the deck shack minutes later, swaying slightly, pausing for a moment before the second sugar bin where Gunnar's body lay like great salted fish, I felt my stomach cave in even further. I had expected someone else.

He took a good slug from the fifth of whiskey that rested in his huge hand like a baby's bottle and stared at absolutely nothing at all. Then he made a kind of sliding shuffle toward his nest behind the stacked sugar bags a few yards from the bin. I heard him rustle around for a moment among the paper bags and then in the silence of the room I heard the bottle tip once more. Then I heard nothing.

I didn't move. I thought about LOTTO. I thought that if Vidar could show up in this precise circumstance in my life and at this very time and place, then I should have no trouble with six numbers out of forty eight when I got back to Seattle. But then I wondered if he would even try to help me if I needed it, or even if he could. But I didn't have long to think about that.

I heard the wheezing, sweaty grunting when he was at the bottom of the ladder leading from the factory. First a little groan of irritation and then the massive bald head appeared like a rising moon from the opening. Then the sloping shoulders encased in the bright white of a cook's uniform, then the impossibly wide black polyester pants, then the rest of him. He paused at the top and took a white handkerchief from his pocket and wiped the sweat from his face. He put away the handkerchief and stood, immobile. Silent, listening. He looked carefully toward the deck shack and then crept up to the entrance with more grace than I could have imagined, and peered inside. Empty. Satisfied, he turned to the far wall and made a soft humming sound as he approached the bin. As he passed within three feet I realized he was humming something. Something my mother used to hum while she held me in her lap, after I had taken a fall, or whenever I was sad.

Hush, little baby, don't make a sound,
Momma's gonna buy you a mockingbird,
And if that mockingbird won't sing,
Momma's gonna buy you a diamond ring.

The humming got louder as he reached into the bin and pushed away the sugar and salt. Then it stopped. He grunted a little, and then in a single movement he pulled Gunnar's stiff and lifeless form from the salt like it was a chunk of redfish fillet. That's when I stood up.

The steel bar felt cool in my sweaty hand and I rested it against a stack of sugar bags.

"Forget it, Tonni. Just let it go."

He turned and dropped Gunnar's body and made a hissing sound like big snapping turtle when you wave a stick in front it. Then his face went through some changes I didn't think were possible on a human being. He was way past rational.

The last emotion that settled in his eyes was sadness. And pity, I felt. His voice was smooth and light and southern, like a warm breeze. He said, "Oh ... I'm so unhappy that you are here, Fish."

The salt encrusted form of the dead old man lied crumpled at his feet. I felt a sudden rush of anger through my fear. I said, "You sick sonofabitch. How'd you kill him, anyway, Tonni? Strangled him in his sleep?"

He opened his mouth and made a wheeze. I think it was a laugh. "It was an ... accident!" *Wheeeeeeze.* "An accident. I only wanted to make him sick." His face turned angry for a moment. "He wouldn't get sick enough! The engineer said ... the engineer said ... oh, but why should I tell you. You're a nice boy, but ..." he trailed off and looked at me and I had no words for what I saw in his eyes.

Chapter 20

I gripped the steel bar. He ignored it. He took a step toward me and stopped. There was a silence, and my voice filled it.

"Why? Why, Tonni? Why kill the old man? What could it possibly accomplish?"

His face twisted in rage. "It accomplished plenty, *peanut*. Plenty. You ... you can't possibly know what it meant -- means. And shall I tell you why?"

My mouth was dry. I tried to swallow. "Tell me."

"Because ... you know nothing of *love*." He leaned on the last word and took another step. This time he was coming.

I smashed the steel rod into the floor and let my terror out in a scream that should have awakened Gunnar. But it only roused the deck boss, which was enough for me. The big Viking shuffled and poked a head from his nest. He stared at a moment at the huge form of the cook and then the misshapen body curled on the floor and then he growled like a bear before he lunged.

I raised the steel bar and tried to cover the distance before they clashed but on the way I saw a streak of light in Tonni's hand and Vidar's neck snap back in an explosion of red. There was a split second of complete stillness that I'll never forget -- Tonni's thick bulk spread-eagled and hunched slightly forward like an umpire calling SAFE, his right hand closest to me holding a bloody razor, and Vidar, suspended in a moment of equilibrium, on his knees, his neck open like a wide crimson smile, then falling forward in slow motion forward at Tonni's feet.

I swung the bar and knocked the razor from the steward's hand. I heard the bosun making inhuman sounds, and saw from the corner of my eye a red pool spreading fanlike from his chin across the spilled sugar covering the floor. Then I stepped forward and swung at the leering grin before me, but he was fast. Faster than me. He grabbed my wrist on the way down and with a heavy twist I felt a shock of pain move straight up my arm to the shoulder. I fell with the momentum and heard the steel clatter against the deck just a moment before I landed on a low pile of bags. I heard him laughing and felt the crush of his ham-like forearm against my right arm and throat. I looked up at him and struggled like a pinned fly as he held me and laughed.

With his left hand he grabbed fifty pound bags from nearby and slapped them on top of my legs. One, two, three, then against my waist, then more bags on top of my legs. I threw hooked, useless punches with my left toward his heavy jowls but he laughed and piled on more bags with a single powerful arm. He grabbed my left wrist with a free hand and slammed it into the deck and I left it there, more concerned with my ability to breathe. He maintained pressure on my throat and piled bags on my left arm. Then he leaned back and slammed some bags into my chest, then he released me. I was pinned but I took deep, grateful breaths. He added more bags, covering me four or five high on every part of my body except my face. Then he stood up and sucked great lung fulls of air, wheezing in the sudden silence.

He stood for a while and surveyed the room. Gunnar lay where he had dropped him, a salted, slimy pile of flesh and clothing. The great length of Vidar stretched out fully and facedown beside me, silent in his growing pool of blood. Tonni's face continued to change, and small dog-like noises, louder than the wheezing, came from the back of his throat. I watched him move slowly in the direction of the razor that lay bloody and shining on an empty paper bag.

Everyone says that your life flashes before your eyes at that moment. Not mine. I was aware only of the scrunching sound of wide black sneakers against the crusted sugar on the floor, the glare from the neon bulb above, and the incessant pounding of blood against the inside of my skull.

When he returned he was humming again. The same tune. A crazy thought streaked through my mind that this was the song my mother sang when they placed me against her breast for the first time. I had the irrational notion that if I could die believing this, my life would fit together like a sublime puzzle.

His face appeared directly above mine, a bloody, sweating planet. A single drop of liquid fell from his chin and landed just below my left ear. He stared at me for what seemed an hour and I watched with morbid fascination as his face changed to reflect his madness. Then he glanced at the corpses again and the noises from his throat grew to plaintive wailings. I saw him carefully fold the razor, and I heard myself exhale loudly.

I started to speak but he put his fingers to his lips and I saw the smile grow around them. A kind smile. An infinitely loving, and completely insane smile.

He reached toward the pool of blood and touched his index and middle fingers until they were red and dripping. His eyes were wide, distant, unfocused. Then I tasted salt and felt the heat of Vidar's blood as he smeared my lips. His smile increased.

"Such ... such a beautiful boy. I hope ... I hope one day that you may discover the joys ..." he giggled, " ... the joys of love."

Then his face descended slowly like a falling moon and I shut my eyes. I felt his fat lips like grubs against mine and he smelled and tasted exactly like I would imagine death to smell and taste. Then he was gone.

21

I saw Taj enter the room from the deck shack about fifteen minutes later. He didn't notice me. I was having a hard time getting air under the weight of the bags but I managed to start yelling before he could react to the carnage in the room. He was shaking as he pulled the bags off.

Taj started with a question but I cut him off. "We've got to get to Jon! Was he at the fire?"

"Uh huh. He was right in there with Martin and me. Was mostly smoke. Somebody lit a hundred rolls of paper towels. But Jesus, Fish, what happened here? Who was it?"

"Tonni."

"Tonni!"

"Yeah. Look, where's the captain right now?"

Taj removed the last couple of bags and helped me up. I felt like my body was one big bruise. He said, "Up to his room to take a shower and change, I think. He have anything to do with this?"

"Sure does. But he doesn't know it. Let's go."

I started at a dead run and Taj followed.

There was a cold stone in the bottom of my gut as we hurried upward. I had a feeling I'd been lying helpless for too long to prevent what would happen between Tonni and the person he had loved and hated to the point of madness. When I saw the door to Jon's cabin swinging on a single hinge I knew I was right.

First we heard the lullaby. When we appeared at the doorway Tonni didn't even look up. He sat on the captain's wide sofa and sung in a soft, pure voice. His massive belly hung between a pair of stump-like legs. In his arms was the naked body of the captain, still wet from the shower, his neck twisted at an impossible angle. Jon's clear blue eyes stared at a point far past Tonni's shoulder, and his mouth hung open in a parody of a boyish grin. Tonni rocked back and forth and sang.

"Hush little baby, don't say a word
Daddy's gonna buy you a mockingbird
And if that mockingbird don't sing
Daddy's gonna buy you a diamond ring
And if that diamond ring don't shine
Daddy's gonna buy you a Clementine"

Each time the verse changed a little until the singing trailed off altogether, and he bowed his head, lips pressed tight and tears dripping off his chin and onto the Captain's chest. The room felt like a vacuum of silence and pain.

22

He wouldn't move from the couch and he wouldn't let go of the captain. He didn't even acknowledge us as we tied his limbs and body tightly to the sofa.

Martin posted a pair of factory foremen by the door but it was clear the man wasn't going anywhere. He remained lost in a private world of sorrow and madness.

Hastings was nowhere to be found. I had an educated guess as to what had happened. The engineer must have received the fax from my ex-wife, panicked, and went straight to Tonni. The steward had to get rid of him. He probably lured him onto one of the upper decks. At any point outside the accommodation you are three steps from the railing. No one would have heard the body hit the water.

At three-thirty I knocked on Monique's door. I was exhausted, and I must have looked like death. In a tired rush I told them what had happened. We lay down together on the cushioned floor. As they drew the story from me I held both of them against a chill that had grown inside me.

"A little while ago, " I told them, "Martin found thirty packets of scopolamine in Tonni's room. He must have started poisoning the fishmaster from the first day of the trip. Gunnar got sick, but he wouldn't stop fishing. That's when Tonni decided to kill him. Tonni told me it was an accident, but I know he was lying."

"How do you know?" asked Alani.

"Because that night I went to see him about your schedule, when he was cutting the captain's hair, he asked me about moving the groceries. He had it planned perfectly. He would kill Gunnar in his bed and move the body, and Steve would release the skiff. They did it right under my nose. That night, as we worked on the bow, they were down in the freezer. I couldn't see both of them at the same time. I just assumed that one was off to the side, receiving the frozen boxes.

When Steve returned from the skiff, he took Tonni's place. Then Tonni must have killed Gunnar and moved the body to the sugar room. It was damned clever -- moving the groceries gave him and alibi and kept Taj and me out of the deck shack."

Monique sat quietly next to me and listened. Collecting another story. Alani looked at me in disbelief. She said, "They were that desperate to have an American fishmaster?"

"No. Not exactly. It just so happened that placing Jon in the captain's chair would serve both their purposes. We know that

Hastings wanted to Americanize the ship, but Tonni was motivated by something much stronger. He was passionately in love with the captain. It destroyed him to see how little power Jon really had. This was an opportunity to use Hastings' nationalism and genius with computers to place the man he loved in power. But things went wrong."

"I guess so," said Monique.

"Gunnar wouldn't stop fishing, and the office wouldn't listen to Hastings' suggestions to have him replaced. So Tonni decided to force the issue. But when Jon took over, he really took over. He stopped living under Tonni's thumb. Taj listened to a fight between them near the incinerator room one day. And you mentioned that Tonni started having bad mood swings."

"Yeah. He was terrible the last couple of days."

"He was starting to crack against the pressure. The guy he was in love with was spurning him, Hastings must have told him that I had found out about the sonar, and Steve was showing signs of remorse. He must have felt that Steve was the weakest link. So he silenced him."

"My God, Fish, why didn't he kill you?"

"He almost did," I said. " But something happened. I saw it come across his face -- the realization that it was over, maybe, except for one thing. His only thoughts were toward Jon at the moment he was looking at me. Maybe it was just a moment of clarity where he realized that everything he had tried to create was in ashes around him.

"I think he just liked you," said Monique, smiling a little.

"Yeah ...", said Alani. "Pays off to be nice, I guess."

"Hah! Just pure luck. But when he left me alive I knew that Jon was as good as dead."

Alani shuddered against me and pulled me closer. I felt Monique's cool stillness against my shoulder. Long after I heard the steady breathing of the women, my eyes stared at images of death. and violence in the darkness.

23

In the gray room, surrounded with the scent of old coffee, cigarettes, and my own sweat, I opened my eyes and found the face of the person who had asked me to tell this story. What was the name ... Chilton, I think. He was staring at me. There were bags under his eyes that hung like gray curtains, and he pulled long on a cigarette before I spoke. He spoke in a flat, bored voice with a hint of rasp.

"Mr. Saxon, I have recorded your statement. We are prepared to release you at this point, but we are asking that you stay within reach for the next two weeks, in case we have questions."

I didn't ask him to define "within reach" and said nothing as they led me to another room where they took blood samples from my hands a third time. The mood seemed different, or maybe it was just me, telling the story for what I imagined would be the last time, and feeling free from it. They let me take a shower in the police locker room and I was able to pull some clean clothes from my duffel. I was driven to a hotel later that morning and I slept a dead black sleep the likes of which I never before knew. The next morning they put me on a plane back to the Aleutians.

The Dutch Harbor airport is a single room, concrete building with a short runway that ends abruptly at the water's edge. It's
the kind of facility you might expect to find in a place like Belize, certainly not in one of the richest fishing ports in the world.

I arrived in a new Chevy van, the island's idea of a taxi. Martin, Taj, Alani and Monique were there to meet me. Martin fell in between Alani and Monique and chatted while I sidled up to my partner. He and the girls had their bags packed and tickets in their hands. They were taking the plane I came in on back to the mainland.

"Sure you don't want to change your mind, Taj? You'll make a hell of a deck boss."

The Somoan grinned. "Sorry, *bra*. You know I got other ideas."

I looked at the ground and smiled. "Gonna be a cop. I can't believe it."

"I can hardly believe it myself. Don't know what my *Ta'ma* gonna say." Then his face turned serious. "Fish, I saw somethin these past few days. Only way I can explain it is to call it evil. Maybe it's crazy, but bein a cop might be a way to do somethin about it."

"Yeah. Might be. Maybe you'll learn the right way to do it. God knows I fucked it up. If we'd a been pros, maybe it'd turned out a lot different."

"Maybe, *bra*. But we did what we could."

We had reached the ticket line. I stuck out a hand. His grip was firm and his eyes clear.

I said, "Later, Taj. Hope I see you again."

"Oh, I think you might. If I make it through the academy, I'm askin for the Dutch Harbor post."

"Hah! You'll get it. Doubt anybody else wants to work out here, " I said.

Then he nodded and stepped up to the ticket counter.

Alani and Monique stood together at the end of the line. We hugged and made a small triangle. I dried Alani's cheeks with the sleeve of my sweatshirt and kissed her on the forehead. Monique smiled warmly and placed a cool hand behind my neck.

She said, "Sure you're making the right decision?"

I glanced for a moment at the tarmac outside. A wind was blowing a fine snow across the water. Small drifts had begun to form around the wheels of the waiting plane.

I said, "Damned if I know."

She laughed and Alani smiled. I saw Martin waiting patiently at the door. I kissed them one more time and touched their faces.

We decided to save the ten bucks and walk the half mile back to the dock. I looked at the steep white mountains all around us as we pushed against the wind. Martin and I were engaged in conversation for the entire walk back. We talked about fishing.

Epilogue

Five hours from the Thai mainland there is an island called Ko Tao. On Ao Mae beach just north of Ban Mae Hat you can rent bungalows for about a dollar a night. The breezes come in the afternoon from the west, rustling the squat palmettos that sit everywhere like small green Buddhas.

I am sitting in the shade on a lounge chair made from bamboo poles and woven palm leaves. Alani and Monique are standing knee-deep in the clear green water. They are holding hands and looking out toward where the light blue of the distant sky meets the line of dark water. They are standing immobile, like statues, and the sea moves gently around their legs.

I reach under my chair to a cardboard case and pull a thick blue book onto my lap. I take a deep breath and smell the rich, sweet scent of flowers. I open and begin to read.

Afterward

I worked in the Bering Sea from 1989 to 1998. Those ten years were both forming and fascinating for me in many ways. I mainly worked on large factory trawlers, and mainly for a single company, where I was lucky enough to rise in rank from processor to First Mate.

I quit just after gaining my Captain's license, and just before I would have sailed as master of the vessel. During those ten years, though, I worked at just about every job a person could on those boats that employed up to 150 people at a time. For those readers who work in the industry now, it's worth mentioning that when this book was written, the industry was "Olympic" in nature – that is, there was a race for fish. No quotas, and every moment counted. This is no longer the case – and that's probably a good thing.

In 1993, I was a deckhand, and wrote this novel in a furious rush while on land for a 25 day period. I never attempted to publish it, until now. It's a small slice of a much larger experience, but it provides a fictional window, however narrow, into our lives, out there in the Bering Sea, at that time.

Owen Scott

August, 2010

www.ingramcontent.com/pod-product-compliance
Lightning Source LLC
Chambersburg PA
CBHW060323260626
47160CB00007B/2660